THE
MOST
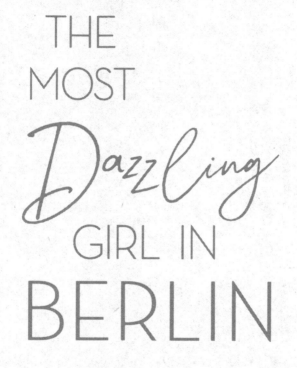
GIRL IN
BERLIN

THE MOST

Dazzling

GIRL IN

BERLIN

BY KIP WILSON

VERSIFY

AN IMPRINT OF HARPERCOLLINSPUBLISHERS

Versify® is an imprint of HarperCollins Publishers.

The Most Dazzling Girl in Berlin
Copyright © 2022 by Kip Wilson
For information address HarperCollins Children's Books, a division of
HarperCollins Publishers, 195 Broadway, New York, NY 10007.
www.epicreads.com

ISBN: 978-0-35-844890-7

Typography by Samira Iravani

1 2022

First Edition

For Monica

February 1932

FEBRUARY 25, 1932
RELEASED

I've looked forward to
            leaving
the orphanage run by
the Gray Order of
Sisters of
the Holy Elisabeth

        for eight long years

and even though I'm walking
away today with only a
handful of Reichsmark coins
in my pocket and

nothing

else except the rough sack of a
dress and woolen coat I'm wearing

I'm marching
out the door
without
looking
back.

LESSON LEARNED

When Gretchen left

six months
one week
and two days ago

she didn't

      look back
      come back
      drop me a line

not even a single
Liebe Hilde

though she promised

           she would.

DREAMING BIG

Gretchen was always
full of
plans

plans to make it big on

the silver screen like
Marlene Dietrich

plans to wrap
herself with pearls, paint
herself with lipstick

plans I should have seen
didn't
include me.

PLANS

I've been running
through my own options
ever since Gretchen left to
audition for the next
Fritz Lang picture

    where she's probably working now
        which is why she probably
    never wrote (probably).

I can't work in
the pictures, not with my
    towering height
    skinny limbs
    mud-brown hair

          crooked teeth
not that I have any interest
in getting in front of a
          camera, director, audience
for any
reason
at all.

No, my plans are much
less lofty
          cashier
          shopgirl
          waitress
anything that will earn
me some money
for a bed,
four walls of my
own, a small
corner I can
finally call
home.

DESTINATION

I'm heading toward
the shops on Müllerstraße

just a few blocks away from
the orphanage

but *home* appears
in my thoughts, halting
me in my tracks

  the neighborhood of Schöneberg
  the small flat I shared with Mutti
  the sound of her velvety voice
    whispering *Hildegard* as she
    kissed me good night.

Home for my first ten years.

Nothing like the
sterile rows of
beds, the long tables and
hard benches for
meals of gray porridge,
stale bread, watery broth.

  Home
    Mutti
      Schöneberg.

I take a step forward, then
stop once more. Surely

there are as many opportunities
in Schöneberg as here.

I clatter down the stairs
to the U-Bahn, surrender
twenty-five Pfennig, enter
the train that whisks
me clear across Berlin to
my old neighborhood.

I'd rather start off in a place that
already feels like home.

OLD HAUNTS

I'm a ghost, stepping

    off the train
    out of the station
    across Nollendorfplatz.

No one notices me gliding
down the block toward my old
neighborhood, my invisible mother
beside me, clutching my hand, leading
the way along Kleiststraße
toward Tauentzienstraße to

Herr Koch's Gemüseladen, where
we used to buy

    potatoes
    turnips
    onions.

I run a fingertip over
the wooden counter that used
to stand at eye level

but before I can ask
Herr Koch if he can use
an extra pair of hands, the same old
man who used to slip an extra
potato in our basket with a smile

takes one look at my rumpled
dress, my ratty hair, shakes
his head, points to the door.
                Raus!

My face flames as I brush
past paying customers and
out to the street, where
lost people like me
        shuffle
                in front of shops

sit
> next to hats waiting for coins

huddle
> in grimy alleys.

I must try harder.

FROM KADEWE TO KU'DAMM

I pass by the immense display
windows of KaDeWe
> Kaufhaus des Westens

once again feeling
Mutti's hand gripping
mine, pulling
me forward to examine
the lovely wares.

I can't even imagine
marching inside someplace so
dazzling to ask for work
> especially

when all my reflection shows
is my ragged appearance.

I run my fingers over
flyaway strands escaping
my chin-length bob, straighten

my dress, encourage
myself by humming a favorite
childhood song

Alle meine Entchen
schwimmen auf dem See

glance across the street
at the elegant, overflowing
Romanisches Café beside
the Kaiser-Wilhelm-Gedächtnis-Kirche
its spire poking
the heavens like
a sharp needle
head down Ku'Damm
    Kurfürstendamm
      the most stylish boulevard in all Berlin
getting more and more

          intimidated

with each door I pass

      intimidated

but not

defeated.

REJECTED

I try again
and again
and again
and again

making my way toward the
southern end of Schöneberg

but even at Herr Lachmann's
Buchladen

       the first and only
       bookstore I've ever known

I don't get any further.

When I ask for work, remind
him of my visits in the past, his
lips whisper *Sorry*, hand gestures
to the *Berliner Tageblatt* spread
over the counter with
the dismal headline
       SIX MILLION OUT OF WORK

head shakes, finger points
       away, away, away

and I wonder
how I'm going
to find my way in this

cold
hard
world.

LAST-DITCH EFFORT

Day turns to night
my feet grow weary
walking in circles
but still I continue
      until
the cozy Café Leon beckons
with glowing golden light over
bursting-full tables tended
by one very occupied waiter.

I slip inside, step
up to the counter, clear
my throat.

     Might you need an
     additional waitress?

Desperate, harried,
the manager whips
his head toward
me at the sound of my
voice, his eyes
full of interest.

But after one look at
what I have to offer
he frowns, shakes
his head *nein.*

It's not personal, he lies.
I simply can't afford
to hire any help.

At least that
last part
rings
true.

I nod, wrap
my arms around
myself, head back
out into the night.

BEDTIME

My stomach empty
spirit broken

I look for a place to rest in
Viktoria-Luise-Platz

a small park where
Mutti used to bring me to play.

Our old flat overlooks
the fountain, the trees, the grass

and I try to imagine running
back home

try to imagine having
somewhere to go

and I have to blink back
my tears.

The benches look
too hard, too public

especially with brown-shirted soldiers
patrolling the area in pairs

roughing up
anyone they feel like

so I opt for the moss-covered
ground beside a linden tree

pulling my coat
close

hoping to steal
some much-needed sleep

because nothing else can take
today's failure away.

FEBRUARY 26, 1932
MY FUTURE

Another day with
nothing
to show for it but
      sore feet
      more job rejections
      my last Reichsmark spent
on bread and

when the day finally comes
to a close, an insistent rain
begins
to
fall.

I stand

      umbrella-less

in Motzstraße

          drip
    drip
              dripping

and all I want to
do in this moment is sit

somewhere, warm
myself, dry
my skin, not worry
about what's to come
next.

BIRDSONG

This
rain, this
street, this
neighborhood make
familiar words bubble
up in my mind, words
Mutti and I sang
whenever it rained
words that slip
out of my own mouth now.

> *Regentropfen*
> *die an mein Fenster klopfen*

and I continue singing
the whole tune until
the rain mingles
with tears because even now

eight years since
Mutti left this earth

　　　stolen from me
　　　by the fever
　　　and cough
　　　and nightmare
　　　　　of influenza

her voice still rings
clear and sweet
as a goldfinch in
my mind and in
my own voice
whenever
I think
of her.

MEMORY

It was always just the two of us
together in the flat

　　　at least
　　　since I was born

a single framed photograph
of a man in uniform

        the only evidence
        of the father

who never even got to
hold me in his arms.

A REALIZATION

With no one
to depend on
but myself and

no luck finding
a job, a home
of my own

I might have to
permanently join those poor
lost souls on the streets and
it's night now and
I have nowhere
to go and
I am already so
so broken.

TWINKLING LIGHTS

At the end of the block, bright
lights wink at me, beckoning
me forward like the North Star.

I follow those lights right up to
a gleaming glass door
the sign announcing
the establishment as
                    Café Lila

the thrum of
          music
          laughter
          conversation
echoing from inside.

Mutti's hand drops
mine, gives
me a push.

EYES WIDE

Music.

Beyond the door
a thick velvet curtain

my fingertips lingering
on the heavy cloth
beyond that
a fairy-tale land.

Partygoers swig
champagne, inhale
cigarette smoke, wrap their
arms around one another
like today is all of
their birthdays at once
dancing, roaring, grinning
all the while.

The sisters would
    not
approve of this
but I am not
one of the sisters.

I hold my breath and wish
to become
one
of these
red-lipped women

dressed in
bright colors, short skirts,

each and every one of them
beaming like their
lives depend
on their bliss.

My own dripping
form makes me

stand
out

like an alley rat, making
me wonder
if I could somehow fade
into the background
or perhaps
run away.

BUTTERFLY GIRL

I turn back
toward the door and in
that very moment collide
with a girl
I tower over, her
perfectly coiffed bob
every bit as dark as

mine but the
exact opposite in
its perfection.

Where are you off to, Liebchen?
The party's this way.

And she takes
me by the hand, takes
me under her wing, takes
me to the bar, where she grabs
a towel, runs
it over my hair, hands
me my first ever glass
of champagne.

Has anyone ever told you you're
the spitting image of Louise Brooks?
Those immense eyes!
And such a waifish look!
She grabs my chin and grins.
Now — what did you say
your name was?

It's Hildegard. Hilde. I mumble
to hide my imperfect teeth.

Her smile overwhelms, and
I can barely squeak
out a *danke*.

I'm Rosa. She nods
this rose-colored butterfly
and before I can manage
anything else, she plants
a kiss on my cheek, tells
me to enjoy
the show, flits off.

This evening is
looking up.

UNEXPECTED

I'm sipping
champagne I can't
pay for, trying
to blend in when the
phonograph music cuts
out, the
lights dim, the
crowd hoots, and all
attention shifts to
the stage at the
front of the room.

Rosa reappears
wearing
nothing more than

stockings
a tiny skirt
tight vest

barely concealing
moon-white breasts.

The sisters would not
approve.

       Most decidedly not.

A high-pitched cheer rises from
a man in shirtsleeves and suspenders
at the bar

but after a second glance

         at a chin-length curl cascading
         forward over his heart-shaped
            feminine
         face

the only thing clear to me
is that all the lines here
are blurred
    or perhaps
they don't even apply.

My gaze sweeps
the room, taking a
closer look at
all manner of people

women in dresses
men in dresses
women in trousers

and those somewhere
in between
who defy definition

like the slim, attractive person in a suit
short hair slicked back
emerging from the wings
heading for the piano

everyone out
in the open

and I already adore
this place and
these people and
the freedom
it offers
us all.

SHOWTIME

Once the pianist sits and
begins tickling the ivories

Rosa steals
the spotlight
dancing, gliding, singing

so sure of
      her body
      her voice
      herself

with
such a vibrant

           red-lipstick smile
              such seductive winks of
       her long, lovely lashes
                directed at
           several young women
              up front

that all I want to do
is stand
next to her, stare
into those deep brown

eyes of hers, soak
up some of
that magnetism.

ATTRACTION

As if in answer
to my thoughts

at a table near
the stage, two women lean
toward each other, wrap
arms around each other's waists
languidly, leisurely, lovingly

making
me think fleetingly
      of Gretchen

less fleetingly
         of Rosa

making
me wish
nothing more
than to stay.

CIGARETTE BREAK

After a rip-roaring
performance of a good
half dozen songs
already close to my heart

      Rosa blows
              kisses to the crowd,
                      disappears
      backstage.

I've just finished
my champagne, just given up
hope that she'll
come back out when
she reappears
at my side, cigarette dangling
from her smile.

                    Sorry I don't have time to talk now!
                    She hollers over the din, stubs
                    out her cigarette, grabs
                    a tray full of drinks.
                    Our other girl flew the coop
                    so I need to cover her tables tonight too.

I can barely believe
my ears, my luck,

and before I lose
          my nerve
I open my mouth.

          I was looking for work
          as a waitress just today!

She gasps
with delight, sets
the tray back on the bar, grasps
my arm, waves to the
regal, silver-haired woman
pouring drinks, announces,

               Brigitte! I've found
               our new girl!

Before anyone can object,
approve, otherwise comment,
I take the tray, follow
Rosa's pointed finger to
the closest table, begin
serving drinks like
I've done it my
whole life.

ANOTHER ROUND

I don't think I've
      ever
moved so fast
with such purpose
            to the tables
            back to the bar
            to the floor

            tables
bar
      floor

round and round
so fast that I even lose
sight of
      Rosa
until the lights dim
again and she emerges
on the stage for
one more set of songs.

With all attention rightly on
her in the
      spotlight
I retreat to the bar, exhale.
                Well done. Behind the bar,
                Brigitte nods her sleek, silver head.

Payday's Friday if you can
keep it up.

I blink.
    Today?

          You'll be paid
          next week, of course.

Of course.

I'm thrilled
at this opportunity but
already exhausted at
the idea of waiting

one
more
week

before I can

      eat

sleep

        sing

in a room of
my own.

Still, I'm so relieved that
this job is mine that I burst
into a smile.

>   *Jawohl!* I nod.
>   *Danke!*

And just like that
I turn, make
use of my height, scan
the room for
anyone needing attention
           like I own the place
instead of
           it owning me.

THE WEE MORNING HOURS

Adrenaline keeps me
                 running
when my body's used to
                 sleeping
until things finally quiet down
     stage lights off

                piano pushed to the side
                audience heading
                                home.

I do everything I imagine
Brigitte would tell
me to do, picking up
empty glasses, pushing in
wayward chairs, wiping down
tables, staying
one step ahead.

After kissing a handful of
pretty patrons good-bye, Rosa approaches
            through this crimson-walled
            blue-smoked hall

bending
close as if to tell
me a secret.

                        You did a marvelous job tonight.
                        Her voice low and silky
                                her lips brushing my ear.
                        Glad to hear you'll be back.

I swallow.
I'm glad to have the job.

Glad to be here,
glad to be out of the rain,
glad to be with you,
I don't say.

Well, I guess we're through.
She takes my cloth, returns
it to the bar, pulls
on her coat and hat, picks
up her umbrella, pocketbook.
Ready?

I wish
for a way to curl
up here for the night
     but
Brigitte's already shut
off the main lights, locked
up out back and now stands
tallying cash at
the bar, raising
a hand in farewell.

I've no choice but
     pretend
I have somewhere
to go.

DESTINATION UNKNOWN

By the time we step into
the street, the rain's tapered off
to a light drizzle, but still Rosa pops
her umbrella open, lifts
it over our heads.

Where to? she asks as though
her umbrella's the taxicab that
will take me home.

The question catches
me off guard and I freeze,
my mind as empty
as the street around us.

Which way?
She halts. *You do have a bed
somewhere, don't you?*
Her gaze scans the alleys
and shadows around us.

I . . .

Well. Rosa tilts her head. *Well.
You really are a waif, poor thing.
You can come home with me tonight.*

She nods. *My aunt's used to*
me bringing home strays.
A small laugh escapes her lips.

I picture myself a mangy
alley cat scooped up in
her arms and while it could
      hurt
to admit how needy I am

instead I take one look at this
jolly girl, laugh with her, take
the elbow
          she offers
me.

ROSA'S FLAT

Our arms brush
against each other
      electric
as Rosa tells me what
to expect.

It's my aunt's flat — Tante Esther.

I don't need to ask
where her parents are.

Half our generation lost
fathers to
the Great War
mothers to
influenza, poverty, exhaustion.

It's lovely and with plenty of space
for me to bring a guest.

Of course. The strays.
I build up my
defenses a little
thicker, a little
stronger
        but
her eyes sparkle
her smile sings.

Tante Esther's sure to be asleep now,
but you'll meet her in the morning.

Our footsteps clop
pleasantly over the
sidewalk while our
surroundings gradually turn

        from Schöneberg
        to Charlottenburg

as we cross
Ku'Damm and head down
Fasanenstraße

    where the houses look lovely
          even
in the dark.

           This is it. Rosa gestures
           with her chin to a
           four-story building with a
           pale façade and extracts a
           set of keys
           from her pocketbook.

              Home
              sweet
              home.

THE BEDROOM

We head
up the stairs two
flights to

    another door
    another key

        an oblong object Rosa touches
             to the right of the door

before she leads the way
inside.

We tiptoe
down a short
corridor to a small
room, where she lights
a lamp, bringing the
space to life in a
golden glow

        a wardrobe, vanity, matching nightstand,
        a grand bed, big enough for two.

I blink
shift in my shoes
but Rosa's already setting
down her things, opening
the wardrobe, handing
me a nightgown
her fingers brushing
against mine.

She extracts
her own from under

a pillow, pulls off her
dress right there, pulls
the nightgown over
her soft curves and
            just like that
I'm back
in the orphanage, getting ready
for bed in front
of the other girls.

MEMORY

Identical dresses discarded
identical nightgowns donned

        a chorus of whispers
        a symphony of bedsprings

lights out
door closed.

                Many minutes later
                so many I was almost asleep

        stealthy footsteps crept forward
        in the quiet darkness.

A soft hand on my shoulder
lifted the scratchy blanket

    I wrapped an arm around
    Gretchen's waist, pulled her close

kissing, touching.
Heaven.

INSOMNIA

Tonight with Rosa is nothing
like those secretive nights
of the past with Gretchen.

Tonight we both flop
on the bed

    exhausted

and while Rosa's knocked
out snoring
within minutes

tonight I lie
    awake
my mind jumping

from the joy of being
here in this comfortable
bed with Rosa to

    those other strays who've
    laid their heads on this pillow

to my very conscious effort
to keep every bit of myself

    on my side of
    the invisible line in
    the middle of
    this bed.

FEBRUARY 27, 1932
MORNING

I only realize
I must have finally drifted
off to sleep when I wake
with a start
     under
the warm comforter
     instead
of a scratchy blanket.

Rosa stirs beside me as
sounds of life emerge
down the hall. She sits
up, stretches, rubs
her eyes, smiles.

That'll be Tante Esther.
I'll go say hello.

I burrow
under the comforter
as voices murmur
footsteps patter back
followed by Rosa's voice
from the door.

Time for breakfast!

And like a trolley
                    slamming
into me without warning
I remember the last time
I had a pleasant wake-up
          at home with Mutti

not so very far from
here at all.

BREAKFAST

Rosa's looking
at me strangely
so I bury
my memories
my emotions

                    feigning
          sleepiness, rubbing
                    my eyes, stumbling

out of bed, following
her to breakfast.

Tante Esther already sits
at the table sipping

coffee, eyeing
the two of us as we enter.

Guten Morgen.

Morgen. I return the
greeting, adding, *Tante Esther.*

It wouldn't feel right
to call my host simply Esther.

We called all the sisters
Schwester Maria
Schwester Agnes
Schwester Whoever.

Tante Esther cracks
a smile and
Rosa giggles, slipping
into her seat.

See, I told you she was lovely.

The breakfast conversation
is filled with
long pauses
statements about the weather
a discussion of

the upcoming presidential election
next week, including Tante Esther's opinion on
      the crusty old guard Hindenburg versus
      the Nazi thug Adolf Hitler versus
      the Communist Ernst Thälmann
      versus candidates from
      other, smaller parties
      who might spoil
      the results

   followed by
      uncomfortable questions
        about me

          Where were you living before this?
          You don't have any family at all?

but

when Tante Esther mentions
Anna
      evidently the last
      girl Rosa brought home
Rosa brushes
the comment aside with
a sweep of her hand.

          Ach, Anna was just a little bit of fun.

She shrugs
     at her aunt
but winks
     at me.

And despite my misgivings
     about Anna
     about Rosa
     about the girls she kissed good-bye
          at the club last night
I can't help feeling
a magnetic pull drawing
me to her.

ANTICIPATION

When evening falls
Rosa dresses
for the club, unbuttoning
her everyday blouse and
skirt, pulling a short dress
over her perfect
plumpness as I attempt
to avert my gaze.

She sits
at the vanity, does

her face, her curls
    so lovely.

I perch awkwardly
at the edge of the bed with
    no other clothes to change
    into, no idea how to
    put on makeup, style
    my hair

but

once Rosa's bob is shaped
to perfection, her lips shiny
red, eyebrows drawn, she turns
to me, waves
me over to sit
beside her

and

I close
my eyes, let
her take over
    a soft brush tickling
        my eyelids
    a larger one brushing
        my cheeks

       her warm hand holding
               my chin
and when I open
my eyes again, I look

    nothing

like her but
thankfully nothing
like myself
either.

ON REPEAT

My second night at
Café Lila starts
much like the first

      running from
            the bar to
        the tables
          and back again
     watching
         Rosa flirt
      with pretty girls
        here and there

wondering
                    what it would be like
          if she flirted
          with me
sipping
          champagne
listening
          to lovely music
                    taking it all in.

Brigitte officially introduces
me to Ute

          the perfectly androgynous pianist.

We shake hands and nod
then Ute leans over the bar, plants
a kiss on Brigitte's lips, shatters
her composure.

                    That's my girl! Ute announces.

Brigitte makes a
sound somewhere
between a
          snort and a
harrumph, snaps
a bar towel at
Ute, turns away

but

the hint of
a smile that plays
on her lips shows
without a doubt that

all
kinds
of
love
are
possible
here.

UNCOMFORTABLE

Once we pass the first
rounds of drinks to
patrons
       their bottles
       their glasses
       overflowing

once we take our own sips
from glasses at the bar

Rosa gestures
with her chin toward
the stage, reaches
for my hand.

Ready to join me?

I stumble
choke
freeze.
       On the stage?

Well, sure! You know all the songs.

Rosa looks
me over, registers
my fear, blots
her lips together.

We usually do both, we girls.
Serve drinks and perform.

I shake my
head, dread filling
me heavy as
concrete.
       I...I...

A sigh, a smile, a soft arm

around my shoulders.

Look, don't worry about it for now.
I'll sing alone tonight.
But at some point . . .

The rest of her
sentence hangs
        in the air
thick as the
cigarette smoke
        around us

and I nod,
acknowledging that
I'll need to reckon with
this fate
        at some point
but thankfully
not
today.

MEMORY

After years of private lessons at home

        Mutti brought me along
        to the opera house

for my first audition.

Standing there on the stage
froze me solid for a moment

      yet I managed to sing
        chirping out nightingale notes

    that soothed my soul

until I finished
they asked for a smile

    and one long look at me under the spotlight

      meant my homely mug would never
      grace their stage again.

HOSPITALITY

Though Rosa only invited
me to stay last
night, the invitation
evidently still stands
because when it's closing time
she turns to me with a smile.

Coming?

She teeters
in her heels and
I steady her while
trying not to teeter myself

but we make it
to her home all right
and my second night
there is
          nothing
like the first.

Exhausted
beyond belief
I can barely keep
my eyes open
as I pull on
my nightgown

                    and when

my head hits
          the pillow

I succumb quickly
soon sleeping the sleep
          of the dead.

FEBRUARY 28, 1932
THE BATHTUB

Sunday is bath day and
Tante Esther's flat has its own
lovely bathroom right inside
          something
    I've never seen
       before.

For my whole life until now
     at home with Mutti
     at the orphanage
it was the same
        communal baths
            forever away
down the hall.

So when my turn comes today
I bask in the moment, slipping
     into the warm water
         sliding
my fingertips along
the white porcelain
         gliding
my toes over
the smooth bottom of the tub
         drawing
in a breath at the

luck that plucked me
off the streets and
brought me here to
this glorious
luxurious
home

even if
my stay here
might
only be
fleeting.

RAUS MIT DEN MÄNNERN

The last shimmers of
gray daylight wink
through the
small window above

and a sudden inspiration
makes me grab
the bathing brush, hold
it like a fat microphone,
whisper-sing

Raus mit den Männern

(Out with the men)

a line from one of the songs
Rosa performs last
at Café Lila.

The flat's quiet,
my words tentative,
            nothing
like how Rosa belts
them out at the club
                    but still
            just like always
something's there
some bit of
Mutti's velvety voice
in mine so

I clear
my throat, begin
anew, letting the song spill
over the tub, across the tiles.

        Raus mit den Männern!

The sound of my own voice lifts
me like bath bubbles, untethering

me from this world, sending
me up to the heavens.

The door creaks
open, I splash
under the water,
hide behind
the curtain.

MEMORY

Each morning at the orphanage
before anyone else was awake

    I snuck
    off by myself

        to the washroom
        stepped up to the sink

            to the scratched, warped
            mirror above it

        channeled
        Mutti

    opened
    my mouth

and
sang.

CAUGHT

I peek around
the curtain.

Rosa
        dark head
        poking
into the bathroom
                mouth agape.

                        Was that you?
                        She blinks.
                        Singing?

I stand up, reach for the
towel at the end of
the tub to cover
myself before I step
out.

            Sorry.

                        Whatever for? Rosa steps
                        toward me, surprise still

written in raised eyebrows.
You sing like a nightingale, Hilde.

I pull
the towel closer,
cool rivulets of
bathwater dripping
down my back, wishing
I'd kept
      my mouth
shut.

A TERRIFYING PROPOSITION

Rosa cocks her
head to one side
      eyes sparking
as she takes
me in anew.

*With a voice like that
you really do belong onstage.*

I look
down, bump
into the bathtub, lose
my balance.

Rosa reaches
out a hand to steady
me, smiles
a dazzling
smile.

*I'm sure Brigitte and Ute
will be asking soon
when you're going to perform.*

I know. I shake
my head, the dread
of standing in a spotlight
of being judged for more
than my voice
choking me.
Just not yet.

Rosa sighs, steps back
out
to the corridor.

*Well, come on then.
Let's get ready.*

March 1932

MARCH 4, 1932
DIFFERENCES

It's Friday evening
almost time to get ready
for work
when Rosa says

> *Tante Esther will be calling me*
> *for Shabbat soon. A pause.*
> *Care to join us?*

I blink as
my Catholic upbringing
           thrusts itself
into my thoughts
not even sure what
           Shabbat
would entail.
Sitting on hard benches
in a temple like
at weekly Sunday Mass?

Rosa laughs, answers
my unspoken question.

> *We light candles*
> *say a prayer*
> *share a meal.*

Ideally we observe through Saturday
but Tante Esther knows I have to work.

I respond without
another thought
    I'd love to
thrilled for the chance
to experience
this important part
of Rosa's life
alongside her.

CONNECTION

Tante Esther lights candles
says a blessing
they sing a song

    and it's all so quiet
    and deliberate
    and moving

then Tante Esther shares
small cups of wine
chunks of soft challah

each moment
as important
as the next

and I haven't felt
so at home
in such a long time.

STEPPING OUT

After we finish
Tante Esther retreats
to the sitting room

we retreat
to Rosa's bedroom
prepare ourselves

      for the night ahead.

We share a smile
as we peer into
the mirror

and even after
these nights together
at the club

not to mention the nights
I make myself stay
on my side of the bed

I only feel like
I'm really getting to know
Rosa now

which reminds me that
perhaps I never truly knew
Gretchen at all.

PAYDAY

Another night
another round
another closing time

     and

Brigitte calls
us over to pass
out the weekly pay

     (my first!)

counting thirty Reichsmark
into my open palm.

It's more money
than I've ever held
at once

but

after looking at the
ads in Tante Esther's
newspaper all week

I can already see
it isn't nearly enough to
claim a room of my own.

I glance at
Rosa, afraid to ask
for more hospitality

but

she makes me pocket
my cash, follow
her home.

MARCH 7, 1932
A DAY OFF

The club's closed
on Mondays, meaning
Rosa and I have the whole day
        and night
to ourselves.

I imagine spending
the afternoon
in this glorious flat, listening
to records on the
phonograph, dressing
up with Rosa, nibbling
on whatever's left of
Tante Esther's delicious challah
        from Shabbat.

Not Rosa.

            Well? What shall we do today?
            She taps her foot.

I shrug, clueless.

            Ach, you're no help. She pulls
            on a velvety cloche, slips
            into her woolen coat with

a fur collar, checks
herself in the hall mirror.
Let's see what strikes our fancy, then.

I set the worn cloche she
was kind enough to give
me on my head, hurry
after her.

Outside, the day threatens,
the sky cloudy, air raw,
and already I want to turn
            around,
but Rosa slips
her arm through mine, warming
me in an instant, filling
me with thoughts
        about her
        about me
        even sparking the
                possibility of
        a someday
                us.

PRIVILEGED

Neat row houses shine,
their bright windows

reflections
of happy lives in this perfect
Charlottenburg neighborhood

Perfect if you can ignore
the politically charged
posters plastered on columns:

VOTE HINDENBURG,

THE MAN OF ACTION

— NOT OF WORDS!

GERMANS!

GIVE THE SYSTEM

YOUR ANSWER!

VOTE HITLER!

FIGHT AGAINST HUNGER AND WAR!

VOTE THÄLMANN!

We take
them in, share
a glance, say
nothing, pass
the Ufa Gloria-Palast,
its GESCHLOSSEN sign hung
over the door in red letters — closed
just like the club on Mondays.

I'd love to go to the pictures.
Rosa lets out a wistful sigh.
Mädchen in Uniform *is still playing.*
Look. Have you seen it?

She points at a poster of
a young actress I don't recognize
leaning her head on
another woman's shoulder.
I raise an eyebrow.

Love at a boarding school.
Rosa smiles, sighs wistfully,
            changes the subject.
In a perfect world, each venue
would be open a different night.

In a perfect world, everyone
could afford to go to the cinema.
I can't help
letting the words slip
out.

You're right, of course. Rosa
squeezes my arm. *I'm so lucky.*

Before I can say
anything else, a commotion

at the end of the block
captures
our attention.

BROWNSHIRTS

A crowd's already growing
                spilling
into the street, mostly soldiers
like countless others I've seen
all over Berlin wearing
black boots, brown uniform shirts
carrying rifles, daggers, red Nazi flags
with the spidery Hakenkreuz
        emblazoned
in the center.

No wonder
Tante Esther called
them thugs.

Men like this
scare
me.

> It's the Sturmabteilung.
> The SA. I tug Rosa's arm.
> Let's go the other way.

Nonsense.
A few Brownshirts aren't
going to ruin my day.
Come on, Liebchen.
She flashes her confident smile.

It's impossible
to say no
to that.

We continue, edging
our way past the crowd, as
uniformed men march
forward, chanting
a song with a patriotic ring
to it, but I only catch
a few words

      ... voll Hoffnung ...
      ... für Freiheit ...
      ... für Brot ...

Full of hope.
For freedom.
For bread.

My gaze drifts
from the soldiers to the
rest of the crowd,

hard eyes glittering
against sunken cheeks,
expressions
filled not with
hope
but with
desperation.

People like this
scare me
even more
than the
soldiers.

PARADE

More people spill out of
shops and businesses, sweeping
us along with them, the whole
crowd packed

    tight as a
    cartload of
    sugar beets

with signs peppering
the crowd
VOTE FOR ADOLF HITLER!

What's going on? Rosa asks.

Haven't you heard? A woman
              purses her pale lips.
Things are looking good
for candidate Hitler
for the vote on Sunday.

Rosa brushes the thought aside.
No one's really taking
him seriously, are they?

He's promising
        work
        food
        hope
just what we need.

Rosa and I share
a glance. How can
such a bully
offer anyone true hope?

But before we can respond,
the crowd sweeps
down the block, leaving
us with some breathing space.

Come on, now. Rosa pulls me away.

Let's start this morning again. I know!
Let's go shopping at KaDeWe.
You need a new dress and
I'd love to see you in something
as pretty as you.

My chest halts
mid-breath, cheeks flushing warm
as I can't help but forget
the world around me,
softly sing a line from everyone's
favorite Marlene Dietrich tune

Ich bin von Kopf bis Fuß
auf Liebe eingestellt

and Rosa joins in
and the two of us make
our way down the block
        laughing
        soaring
        arm in arm.

PURE ELEGANCE

After a marvelous time trying
on hats, getting
a spray of Rosa's gardenia

perfume, purchasing
a new dress with a chunk of
my earnings,
we emerge
back onto the street,
  exhausted
   exhilarated.

       Have you ever been
       to Romanisches Café?

She might as well have asked
if I've been to Paris, or the moon.

I shake my head.

       Then it's settled.
       We're going right now.

She sticks
a shapely leg out over
the curb and for a moment
that single leg draws
as much attention
as all the electric lights at
Potsdamer Platz.

But Rosa doesn't even realize
what her leg has done.

In an instant, she speeds
across the street like a
film reel

set to play again, launching

the rest of the world in motion,
including me, dashing
off behind this wonderful,
charming girl.

THE LUXURY OF IT ALL

The coffee arrives
on a silver tray with
a small glass of bubbly water,
two tiny cookies.

Eyes sparkling,
Rosa watches me take
a first sip, her delight at
these marvelous firsts for
me almost as special as
the experience
itself.

Almost.

The same café I hadn't dared
enter when I was looking
for work, and now I'm
a customer.

I can't believe I'm really here.

Waiters in starched uniforms,
customers at nearby tables —
　　　these charmed people
looking
like they belong.

Well, we couldn't do it every day,
but sometimes it pays to splurge.
You only get one life, Hilde.

If only splurging
wouldn't mean depleting
all of my earnings.

Rosa reaches
for my hands,
our gazes meet,
my feelings clicking
into place
like the tumblers
of a lock.

With a broad, red smile, she brings
one of my hands to her mouth,
her soft lips pressing
against my skin.

A flutter passes
through me.
I've never known
anyone so captivating
      not even
            Gretchen.

              My goodness!
              The woman at the next table,
                    mouth wide open.

Her companion
      an older gentleman
passes
a wistful gaze over
our table.

              Herman! she scolds.

Rosa releases
my hand, we share
a mischievous smile, turn
our attention back

to our coffees like
all of this is
       only
a game.

THE LAST HURDLE

In the past couple of weeks,
I've made the acquaintance of
all the main players at Café Lila

    Rosa, of course
    Brigitte, the boss
    Ute, the pianist
    some of the regular customers

        the lovely Vogel sisters
          almost bookends with
          identical blond bobs
          heart-shaped pink lips
        handsy Herr Neumann
          who goes by the name Marta
          on nights when wearing
          a dress
        Katja and Käthe
          a fun-loving pair
            of girlfriends
          both jolly, always good
           for a laugh

  but Friday night I'll finally meet

    Emil

who's been out of town
on business these past weeks

but is perhaps the most
important player here
as he's also known as

the money

so no one has to tell
me that he's
the one I really need
to impress
in order to stay.

BUTTERFLIES

Rosa steps
up to the bar, preps
me for Emil's visit.

*He can be a bit brusque, but
just show him what you can do.*

My fingers tremble and
my breath falters and
Rosa must sense my ballooning
nerves because she lights

a cigarette, places
it to my lips, squeezes
my hand.

Don't you worry, she says.
You'll do absolutely fine.
Although. A pause.
It might help if you could sing
onstage like you did at home.

I frown, draw in the
smoke, exhale.

Like you did at home?
Ute sidles up to me
eyebrow raised.

Hilde's a fantastic singer.
Stage fright. Rosa shrugs.

Only way over it is through it.
Ute claps me on the back.

They're right, of course

but

I'm just not ready

not yet.

A few more moments and
Brigitte's calling out,

Guten Abend, Emil!

to this man who holds
my future in
his hands.

AN INVITATION

Rosa heads
backstage

I load
up my tray with drinks

someone bumps
into my elbow, spilling
droplets from the last
glass of champagne.

I raise an eyebrow, turn.

You're the new girl, right?
A boy, tall and gangly as I am.

I'm Kurt, Emil's assistant.
He wants you at his table. Now.

As quickly as he

    appeared

Kurt dashes

        away

making it clear
that I best make
haste to follow.

KNOCKING KNEES

I speed as quickly
as I can
after Kurt, who makes
a beeline for the
corner table where
a giant of a man who must be

    Emil

sits surveying the
club like a Kaiser with

a much slimmer man
     his clear companion
pressed close
to his elbow.
Both are clean-shaven
hair slicked back
dressed in smart suits
making them look like
     businessmen.

Kurt slips
onto a chair, fades
into the shadows beside
someone else at
Emil's other side.

    A girl.

       A blond china doll

   of a girl

           every bit as
       skinny as I am
          but ten times prettier

    sitting there
         glaring
   at me.

I swallow.

Hilde, is it? You're a scrawny one.
Emil looks me over. *How do you do?*

How do you do? I return,
hoping the tremble in
my voice isn't all that evident,
hoping this girl with
         such evident dislike for me
has no say in whether
I stay
or go.

This is Erich
         real estate tycoon
         Berliner
         love of my life.
The two of them share a smile.
And this here's Lena. He gestures
to the girl. *Your competition.*
Brigitte tells me she offered you a job
but meanwhile I offered one to Lena.
I can only afford one of you
         so we'll have to see
who ends up being more valuable.

My insides spill
to the floor like a
sack of beans.

Emil pulls a cigar from his
pocket

      a toothpick between
      his enormous fingers

lights up
lounges against
Erich's arm over
the back of his chair
while Lena's enormous eyes
                narrow

and I already know that
      between

          my hardworking drive
          and
          her radiant beauty

I have
no chance
whatsoever.

UGLY WORDS

Clumsy
awkward
graceless

The words burned
in my mind ever since I shot
up all at once, towering
over the other girls, leaving
them

      behind

below.

Sometimes it's nice to
be able to see over a
crowd, but mostly it's just

      harder

to move smoothly and
tonight is no exception
especially now that it's

      evident

that this is a
competition.

ON DISPLAY

I'm frozen
in place, unable to

    speak
    think
    move

until I remember Rosa's
advice to show
Emil what I can do.

I am
good
at this.

I flash a smile
    lips closed
pass a glass of
    champagne
to him and Erich, to Kurt, even
to Lena, tell them to

    Enjoy the show!

before bustling
off to other tables

                around

and   around

        and   around

not paying any
mind to the man with
the money and instead

doing
my
very
best.

POP

The night ends
Emil and his
charges leave

      he

          and

that girl

along with

that man and that boy

the air lightens
the mood brightens
I can breathe again.

Rosa kisses
the Vogel sisters good night, changes
into street clothes
I give
the tables a last wipe, push
in the last chairs
Brigitte opens
a bottle of champagne
just for us

which tells me
she might be hoping
I get to stay
too.

MARCH 12, 1932
FRESH AIR

The next afternoon
in the bathroom
    a pounding headache
    cotton-ball mouth
    eyes more pink than white.

I tiptoe back to the
bedroom to collect
my pocketbook.

        Rosa rolls over, squints.
        Where are you off to, Liebchen?

Just out for some fresh air
before work.

        See you at the club then.
        She yawns, rolling to her side,
            draping
        a languid arm over her pillow.

I breathe
in a whiff of
gardenia-scented air from
her sheets.

For the briefest of
moments, I wonder
if she ever wishes
for more, wonder
what it would be
like to share with her
these feelings tumbling
through my mind but
then I remember Gretchen
        how much she hurt me
and I can't, I won't.

I need
this roof over my head
more than I need feelings

even

        shared

ones.

PROMENADE

I wander
from Rosa's well-kept
neighborhood into

a different Berlin
a few blocks away, where

      hard-faced men lurk
          in the shadows
      skinny boys sell
          newspapers on the corner
      Brownshirts roam
          menacing, making
          me keep my distance.

My feet lead me farther
to the lively bustle of
Ku'damm, where
women in furs gaze in windows
eyeing future purchases
               until
a shop catches
my attention, displaying
recordings and a
phonograph in the window.

Music.

A tiny bell rings
when I push
my way inside,
my feet stumbling
over themselves.

Guten Morgen. At that very
moment,
the shopgirl is setting the needle
on a disc.

The music begins
then the lyrics

Es gibt nur ein Berlin!

(There's only one Berlin!)

and the girl and I sigh
in unison. The voice drips
in Berlinerisch
each line shimmering
with confidence.

That voice.
So familiar.

Claire Waldoff's latest.
The shopgirl smiles.
Isn't she just divine?

Of course.
The same singer who made
"Raus mit den Männern" a hit.

But a voice like hers
recorded for the world to hear

only makes me ache
for a recording
of Mutti singing and

I'll

     never

         ever

have one of those,

so I tamp down
my feelings, wonder if
my own voice
might be enough to ever
carry on such a

     powerful

       legacy.

MEMORY

Even after my failed
    audition

Mutti never gave up

        teaching me

        scales, songs, techniques

    never stopped

          believing

    I could follow

          in her footsteps.

DEEP REFLECTION

With a bolt of
confidence, I head back out
    to the street
    around the corner
    down the block.

I spy
my reflection in a
café window, almost laugh
at the stupid grin
on my face, but something else
in the reflection catches
my attention

      a flash of red flapping
      in the breeze.

Across the street behind
me, Nazi flags fly
over a group of Brownshirts
their boots slapping
against the pavement

slapping
the smile
off my face.

PARADE

The SA soldiers aren't alone.
A group of civilians marches
      at their sides.

Men, women, children join

arms, sweep forward, calling
for people to vote tomorrow, carrying
signs like those I saw the other day

VOTE FOR ADOLF HITLER!

and others

THE JEWS ARE OUR MISFORTUNE

pointing
fingers of blame at
cartoonish caricatures.

Jaws clenched, I press
my back against a storefront,
trying to keep

away
          from this crowd

                    away
          from this hate

away
          from what they think
          they know.

FEROCIOUS

I try to steer clear but
the crowd presses
close

> a pack of wolves
> sensing my fear

and I keep my
eyes toward them, my
senses on highest alert

> ready

for fight or flight

> especially when two of them
> > tackle
> a young man holding
> a sign for Thälmann
> > the Communist candidate.

But no one notices
me as they march
past

> flags and signs blaring
> voices booming

the same song about
brown battalions and
hope and freedom and
bread.

Their faces twist
in such fervor that even
attractive faces appear ugly

and in that moment I recognize
one of the faces

     the prettiest
     in the entire
     wave of people.

FAMILIAR

At the tail end of the crowd,
this girl takes

     deliberate

steps beside a man marching
in a uniform from the
Great War.

I crane my neck

studying the blond waves falling
over her rosy-cheeked face.

Without a doubt

it's her

           Emil's charge

      my competition

Lena.

THE WRONG CROWD

After her
nasty glares
at the club
I suppose it
shouldn't be a
surprise to see
that girl shuffling
along with these
scoundrels thrusting
their superiority over
the ones they blame
for Germany's problems.

REHEARSAL

By the time I make it to
Café Lila, Rosa and Ute are
already there, rehearsing
a new song.

I wonder
what it would be like
to simply march
onstage with them and
grab the microphone but

I lose my nerve, step
behind the bar, set
up dozens of glasses for
the first round of the night
my mouth itching
to at least tell
          someone
what I saw on the street.

The song ends.

> *Lovely.* Brigitte nods.
> *But where's Lena? Emil wants*
> *to see her onstage tonight.*
> *He's stopping by early.*

No idea. Rosa shrugs.

*He seems to think
she has not just looks
but talent.*

My ears burn.

Competition

with

talent.

Being a good
waitress isn't enough.

I'll need
to offer something
more.

I swallow, shift
in my shoes.

Enough chitchat, Ute snaps
from behind the piano.
From the top, then.

Ute launches into
"Raus mit den Männern" and
Rosa sings along, dancing

    step, two, three, kick,
                two, three, spin, kick,
   step, two, three

and it's lovely to watch but

I don't think
I can move like
that

    even

if my livelihood
depends on it.

MY COMPETITION

Ute's fingers stumble
over the keys and at the
wings of the stage

    Lena
    stands

in a man's suit
that must've been lying
around with other
costumes backstage

looking exactly like
        Marlene Dietrich
if you can ignore
the frown on
her porcelain face.

This girl clearly hates
being here, hates
all of us, hates
whatever
the Nazis tell
her to hate.

Well, I wouldn't have guessed it.
Emil breaks the silence, standing
at the entrance with Erich,
    taking Lena in.
You make a very handsome boy.

I can't help myself,
I can't stop myself,
and my mouth blurts
out my thought:

A handsome Nazi
is more like it!

SUSPICION

Ute slams a hand
over the low keys.

> *A Nazi?*

> > *The National Socialists*
> > *want to give us*
> > *freedom and bread,* Lena says,
> > then blanches
> > as if remembering
> >   something else
> > before crossing her arms
> >   with a frown.
> > *I want to eat.*

> > *That's enough.* Emil retreats to the
> >   bar,
> > his expression unreadable.
> > *This isn't a political rally.*

The guarded glances among
the others betray

suspicion, making me glad
I spoke up.

None of us knows
Lena
but after seeing her
in that parade

I for one
don't think
we should
trust
her.

LYRICS

Brigitte pours
drinks for Emil and Erich
Ute sits
back down at
the piano, waves
a hand toward
Rosa and Lena.

All right. Lena, do you know the songs?
How about "Das Lila Lied"?

Not that one.

Lena shakes her head.

You can't work in a queer club
and not know that song, Rosa huffs.
Especially this club! Where do you
think Café Lila got its name?

I raise an eyebrow.
I feel as at home here
      as Rosa
but I would never say
such things aloud to
someone like Lena
who clearly doesn't
understand.

Lena frowns, shakes her
    head.
I don't care in the slightest.
I need the money!
She shrugs. *I couldn't find*
a job anywhere else.

Ach, that's rich. Ute frowns.

If you don't know our songs,
you'd better learn.
Rosa catches my gaze and
    her eyes go soft like

a star in a romantic
film.

A wave of heat passes
through my chest and I avert
my eyes

    though

I wish I were confident
enough to storm
the stage and burst
into song
beside
her.

Almost
but not
yet.

AN OPEN WOUND

Instead of "Das Lila Lied,"
they practice "Raus mit den Männern"
again and again.

Lena stumbles through her steps and

her singing isn't any better, flooding
me with relief.

Maybe I have a shot at staying
          after all
even if I never set foot onstage.

The next time her voice squeaks
above range,
I sigh dramatically

          waiting

for someone to criticize her.

Indeed, Emil gets to his feet
and I smirk

until

he points
          at me

spearing
          me with his words,

                    Knock it off!

wiping
         the smile off my face.

The space
                    between
                    us
is a vise grip, tightening
around my throat.

                    It's going to make the club look bad
                    if you call attention to everything
                    she does wrong, Emil growls.

My fault
my failure
my insides
         exposed.

MEMORY

Back

         at the orphanage

lined
up

beside the other girls
in front of parents looking
      to adopt.

They always wanted
pretty, doll-faced girls

    girls like Lena.

No one
    ever
wanted
me.

SHOWTIME

Brigitte's voice rises
from behind the bar, rescues
me from further

    embarrassment.

*We've got these numbers down
as best as we can hope for now.
I'm going to unlock the doors.*

Rosa and Lena head
backstage to get ready
as I scurry to prepare
for a long night.

UNDER SURVEILLANCE

Within a few more
nights, tensions in Berlin
over the elections

    bubble up

        bubble over

and finally

      fizzle out

when results prove
no one has the majority
though Hindenburg comes closest

      PAUL VON HINDENBURG 49.6%

      ADOLF HITLER   30.1%

      ERNST THÄLMANN   13.2%

      THEODOR DUESTERBERG 6.8%

      ADOLF GUSTAV WINTER   0.3%

and a runoff
election is called
for the tenth of April
still weeks away.

We distract
ourselves with
shows that have become
a regular routine

Rosa
        center stage
Lena fading
        into the background
                dancing in Rosa's shadow
                doing a terrible job
                trying to keep up with us
                spilling more drinks than
                        she serves

me trying
        to gather
                the confidence I need
                to sing.

At least Lena matters
as little as I do
at Café Lila

        but

I
still
don't
trust
her.

April 1932

APRIL 1, 1932
SPRING

All Emil says
        is that he'll make up his mind
                about who will stay
                        soon
maybe even
        this week
which could even be
                tonight

but all this indecision feels
like the recent election
with no clear winner
with me hanging on
by my fingertips.

Meanwhile Lent and Easter are over
the runoff looms in a couple of weeks
and Berlin is ready to escape
to gluttony meaning
we are going to be busy.

Brigitte asked us to arrive
early on Friday
to get things ready for
a big night and

127

we hurry to get
there on time.

Partygoers spill
into the streets
        Hausfrauen
                skirts high, necklines low
        veterans passing bottles in alleys
                half-drunk already.

Inside Café Lila
Emil stands at the bar pointing
a thick finger at Brigitte and Ute.

                        You leave Lena to me.
                        Half the Berliners who vote
                        for the Nazis don't even realize
                        what they stand for.

Brigitte clears
her throat, Emil turns
toward us.

                        Guten Abend, girls.
                        Just the two of you?

We nod.

                        We were just talking about

128

your friend Lena.

She's not our friend. I can't help
the words tumbling out of my mouth.

She could be, Kurt says, making
us all look his way in surprise.

Look, I asked around, Emil
says.
*She's bringing her pay home
to a kid sister and father.
A war veteran.*

At least she has a
home and a family.

*Maybe you should give
her more of a chance.*
Kurt crosses his arms.

Emil's round shoulders hunch
        forward
like he actually cares
about us accepting Lena
        (a Nazi)

and it burns me
more than anything

that he wouldn't
act the same way about me

especially when
her acceptance
        equals
my exclusion.

FIZZLED

Lena doesn't arrive
until Rosa and Ute are
ready to rehearse but
when she does, Kurt greets
her with extra heaps of
enthusiasm
        in his voice
        in his eyes
        in his red, red cheeks.

Another point
        for Lena
                        another point
        against me.

                She's here, Ute says. *That's everyone.*

                Good. Listen up, Brigitte

calls from the bar.
With the runoff election
           coming up
people are going to be
letting off steam
           so I want to see
           champagne glasses full
           customers merry
           show spectacular.

If we want a spectacular show, Ute says,
let's do something different.
Lena can sing "Das Lila Lied" tonight
with her pretty face front and center.

A spectacular show.
Her pretty face.
On the night Emil
might decide
my future.

I can't let this happen.
Once again, words tumble
out of my mouth before
I can stop them.

           How about I sing
           "Das Lila Lied"?

Everyone freezes.

Finally! Rosa jumps in.
Hilde will be perfect tonight.

And like that
Brigitte and
Ute and
Emil erupt
in delight
at me stepping
out of my shell
to join the others

and I prepare myself to perform
like my life depends
on it.

SPINNING

The evening kicks
off splendidly
just as Brigitte hoped.

Tables are packed.
Katja and Käthe sit
on other girlfriends' laps, gathering
      their group close.

Each time I run
into Rosa, she grabs
my hands and squeezes and
I don't need to hear
anything over the din to know
she's rooting for me
and my voice tonight

which makes me consider
that once Lena's out
of the picture
other things might
also be possible.

I bounce
from table to table, refilling
glasses with champagne flowing
fast as the Spree River, sharing
a glass with Rosa when I stop
to catch a breath, watching
Lena gulp down her own share
with Kurt, catch him whispering
in her ear.

Beate Vogel pulls
me to her side, her girlfriends offering
sips from never-ending glasses, giggling
at the smattering of lipstick
left behind on the rims.

I whirl

    and whirl

    and whirl

    around the room until

an hour's zoomed past and
before I know it it's showtime.

IN THE SPOTLIGHT

For the first time

    I'm joining them

        I'm part

    of the show

and it all happens so fast

    it's like a dream

        me, touching up my lipstick

stepping onstage

approaching the microphone.

Ute begins to play

a hush falls over the crowd

my mouth opens

I sing

but

before I've even finished the first line

a laugh

rises over the tables

joined by other voices

whooping out amusement

at something

(at me?)

an unexpected slap

in the face.

FAILURE

The music continues
partygoers carry on
but I cannot
and instead

I draw in a breath
        horrified
my voice cracks
my feet step
backward

tears filling
        my eyes
        my heart
        my soul

unable to go on

all my nightmares
        come true.

TAKE TWO

I bolt from the stage
leaving Rosa and Lena
to pick up the pieces

of the performance
I started and left
hanging

hide backstage
long enough to
wipe my eyes
even out my breaths

realize I've got to
hustle back to the floor
if I have any chance
of keeping
this job.

HEARTBREAK

They finish
my number, sing
several others
while I watch
from the sidelines
serving tray in hand
        until
they perform the last
song in the set.

Rosa curtsies, Lena bows

but partygoers get
to their feet, whistling, chanting
    Ein Kuß, ein Kuß
        (A kiss, a kiss).

Everything seems
to stop.

Even after my spectacular failure
    and
even though Emil and Kurt asked
us to give Lena a chance
        despite
        the evidence
        stacked
        against her
surely they didn't mean this
surely of all people
    Kurt
and his burning cheeks didn't
mean this.

Still, Rosa and Lena smile, edging
close, the spotlight focused
on the two of them alone, and I

    can't breathe
    can't look away

as Rosa leans even closer, plants
a peck on Lena's cheek.

My heartbeat thunders
in my chest, but it's over
now, whatever this was

      this nothing

until Rosa swoops
Lena in a dip and presses
a passionate kiss on
her lips

and the howls of
joy from the audience echo
through my head as I stand
there and take it

this blow

to my heart.

MEMORY

Back at the orphanage

      heart splayed open

I waited for word from Gretchen

word that never came

and it hurt

a little less each day

until

I had no feelings left

at all.

SOLITUDE

I pretend
none of this matters
as I step
into the water closet, shut
the door, pace
in front of the toilet
hands trembling.

That terrible girl worming
her way into Café Lila
        and Rosa
kissing her.

I tell myself
it doesn't matter
        I don't matter
so I take
deep breaths, release
my hopes into the air
like untethered
zeppelins

                saying good-bye to

        my insignificant hopes for

                this job

                        this girl

        a home here.

It doesn't matter
I don't matter

to anyone
at all.

EMPTINESS

I shake out

      my arms
      my hands

shaking images
loose

          of Rosa
          kissing Lena

              of Lena marching
              in the parade

and I shake and
I shake and
I need
to get them

          out

of my head
right
now.

I grab

the door handle, prepared
to recognize the truth that

    people like her
        will always win

that what I thought was a
connection between
Rosa and me was

    nothing

more than an act

and now
I have to act
too.

OBLIVIOUS

Things are quieting
down on the floor

    the roar of the crowd settling
to a hum

    the river of conversation trickling
to a stream.

I stride
past Lena and Kurt at
the bar murmuring
fingers touching
heads bent close

      as though what she stands for
      doesn't bother me in the slightest

avoiding Rosa tucked
in the corner jabbering
at Emil
her back to me.

ASSASSINATION

Everyone works together
to clean up, collecting
champagne glasses, rearranging
chairs, wiping
tables, the pleasant sound of
thunk, clink, clink ringing
across the room
      covering up
my inner wish to
scream.

The night complete,

I turn away when
Rosa walks by for
her things, a waft of
gardenia drifting
toward me like

       mustard gas

capable

of
silent
murder.

DECISION

Emil steps
to the bar then, calls

       Lena and me

over to him and
my belly twists
       filling
with butterflies.

            All right, he says.
            I've made my decision.

A pause.

Lena, the job's yours.
Sorry, Hilde.

He extends
a hand to Lena and
the club's smoky air swirls
in front of my face

      choking

me with shock before
I cough, nod, slip
away.

THE END

Rosa says
      nothing
to me, steps
past me behind
the bar to whisper
to Brigitte.

I collect
my cloche
Lena turns

           stops
           stares
           stutters

something new
in her eyes.

Not her usual
disdain, not her usual
contempt, but something
softer, something
sweeter, I realize
with sudden horror.

Something
like

                    pity.

I recoil.

I will walk out
of here

           head high

even if I really feel
like curling into
a ball and

overflowing
with tears.

DARKNESS

I step into
the street alone but
I'm only halfway down
the block when Rosa bursts
out after me calling,

Hilde, wait!

I don't
    wait
    stop
    bat
an eyelash.

Instead I

    pick up the pace
    leave Café Lila behind

    disappear.

DESTINATION UNKNOWN

My chest heaves

from
    running away

    from
        losing my job

from
    Rosa's betrayal

but the only thing on
my mind is escape

    so I keep at it

        running and
        running and
        running until

I realize

    I have no idea

where I am

and no idea

where I'm going.

EAVESDROPPING

I eventually slow
my pace, wander
a few more blocks

until

quiet street sounds

even in the height of night

pull me forward like
a moth.

I'm getting closer to
the Kaiser-Wilhelm-Gedächtnis-Kirche.
For a moment I stand
in the shadow of its spire, consider
saying a rosary of prayers
but nothing can save
me now.

Voices drift over
the sidewalk from a nearby
alley

and I recognize one of them

       but that can't be
            she can't be
                here

so all I can do is

          halt

dead in my tracks

             listen.

THE SHADOWS

A couple
      a young man and
      young woman
steps
out of the alley

him slipping
money into her hand
her slipping
that money into her pocket

and I lean
forward

    listening

        listening.

The girl lets out one of
her unmistakable
laughs

and I gasp
    cover my mouth

    stumble

backward

but it's too late.

Gretchen

    my Gretchen

has
already
seen
me.

EYE CONTACT

Her hazel eyes widen
soft lips open
forming a large O of
surprise
that she just as quickly
       presses
back in place as she shakes
her head, takes
the arm her
companion offers
her, pivots
on the balls of
her feet, lets
him lead her
away

and even when I let
out a cry

    Wait

she doesn't
    slow
        stop
           look
my way.

BOUGHT

Gretchen.
That man
his money burning
into her palm.

She isn't
working in the
pictures, isn't
draped in pearls and
furs, isn't
living the high life
at all.

MY HEART

Gretchen.

All the feelings I thought
I'd buried deeper than

                    the deepest
train tunnel bubble
to the surface

roaring past me
screaming
her
name.

RECKONING

Another uncomfortable
night in the park at
Viktoria-Luise-Platz
filled with all manner of
            downtrodden
individuals curled
up in their own
spaces, making their own
noises, caught up in their own
misery.

My life isn't
going to get
better than this

and

I don't have the means to
make it on my own

      but

at least now I know
      she's
out there
somewhere
too.

APRIL 2, 1932
A PLAN

The next morning

    a chill in the air
    a crick in my neck

I brush myself off, run
my fingers through
my hair, prepare
myself to go look for
        this girl
        my past
        myself.

My mind whirs with
possibilities
at the idea of
                returning
to see if I can catch sight of
her again.

LOOKING UP

I hurry
through the streets toward the
Kaiser-Wilhelm-Gedächtnis-Kirche

the center
of this part of Berlin
with its direct path
to the heavens.

Everything looks
different in
daylight

especially

given my state of
mind last night

but

I locate the alley
soon enough

Gretchen's alley

take a deep breath
step inside.

CLUES

Ten paces in and
the tall brick walls muffle

sounds from the street, closing
me off from the
world.

I hold a breath, listen.

What seems
        quiet
at first fills
with signs of
life

        a rustling
        a shuffling
        the steady drone of sleep

of unfortunate souls like
those in the park.

I tiptoe farther, my
gaze searching hidden
corners, sweeping
surfaces but finding
only a man, a
couple of
boys, no
Gretchen.

I back myself out
to the street before
any of them stir.

I have no desire to
explain what I'm doing
in their home, no
desire to speak with
anyone
but

her.

APRIL 3, 1932
A CALLING

After an exhausting day, another
restless night in the park
I wake with a rumbling
in my belly.

Luckily I have enough
coins in my pocket
for two Brötchen from
the bakery down the block
and I bring them back
to the park for breakfast
hoping the nourishment
will help me figure out
what to do next.

I tear into
the crisp crust
tender insides
     the bready scent making
     my head spin as much
     as the taste
chew each bite
several times to make
it last but
it doesn't
     not long enough.

I'm no closer to knowing
what to do next until
church bells begin tolling

reminding me
it's Sunday
reminding me
of the perfect place
to find Gretchen.

ANSWERING THE CALL

This time I head straight for
the Kaiser-Wilhelm-Gedächtnis-Kirche
        across the street
        from Gretchen's alley

and out there on the sidewalk
the sun blinds
me, making me shade
my eyes with a hand
so I can take in
        the church
                its spire scratching
                the sky
next to the
        Romanisches Café

where I had that elegant
coffee with Rosa.

The sisters

the orphanage

the church.

Gretchen could be
anywhere
but if she wants to be
found
she just might
be there.

GOOD GIRL

I follow others dressed
in their Sunday best
into the church, shuffle
among them past
the first pews, scan
churchgoers for her face.

Several groups of people pepper
the nave, but not the one
I want to find

so

I slip onto a bench in the
last row
                the first soul
        someone might encounter
        upon entering

                sit through the service

and though I try to pay attention to the
        prayers
        hymns
        sermon

all the while I'm considering
my next steps.

GO IN PEACE

The church bells chime
once more when
the service concludes

making the reality sink
in that

Gretchen's

not

      coming.

RESIGNED

One last chime of
the bells and that's it.

I get to my feet, slink
out to the street, heart heavy.

I emerge
      shading my eyes
      from the sun
      once again
only to find

      her

outside

      pacing
      frowning
      trying to make
         up her mind.

CIRCLING

I rush
forward, bursting
with joy

      she steps
      forward, hesitates

I hesitate
at her hesitation

and

we stand
still, observe
each other

      those mischievous hazel eyes
      high cheekbones, dark-blond bob

until it feels
too much like a
dance when what
we really need
is to talk.

I reach
out a hand and

her face relaxes
her body relaxes
she slips
her hand
in mine.

CATCHING UP

Gretchen and I make
our way to
a nearby bench
our eyes
        full
of each other
my mind
                spinning
with questions
that come tumbling
out.

    Why didn't you write?
    What were you doing
        with that man last night?
    Are you still trying to
        work in the pictures?

Her responses are
unspoken.

A shifty gaze

                a guilty look

followed up with

                doubt, disappointment, despair

and all I can do is wrap
my arms around
her, pull
her close.

MEMORY

She always shifted
in my arms

            like she was ready to escape
                that life

                for another, wilder one

            but I always assumed

we'd escape
together.

SILENT PARTNER

Gretchen breaks
free from my embrace, shakes
her head, pushes
me away.

> *Tell me,* I insist.
> *Tell me everything.*

But she refuses
to meet my gaze, sitting
silent instead
      cheeks pink
      tears dripping
          down her face.

COMPOSED

I don't know
what to say, don't
even have
a handkerchief to offer

so

I find myself doing
what I've always done

with Gretchen, spilling
       out my own
             details, my own
                  feelings
of the events that brought
me to this bench, waiting
for her to understand
like no one else can.

Gretchen suddenly sits
up straighter, wipes
her cheeks with her
sleeve, draws
in a breath.

            How terrible of them
            to keep you hanging
            and cut you loose like that.
            At least I'm my own boss.
            Why don't you come
                  home with me?

And who am I
to say no
to that, to her, to
       whatever
help she offers.

THE NEIGHBORHOOD

Gretchen leads
me through streets that
seem grittier, grimier with
each passing block
    crumbling buildings
    ragged clothing hung
        from sagging lines
    filthy faces leering
        from windows, alleys, doorways.

I try not to show my
disgust, my
horror, my
fear

    but

there's nothing I wish
    more
than to be
    anywhere
but here.

HOME

Gretchen's building is
a brown slab of a
tenement like the
others surrounding
it but what hits
me the moment we enter
is an overwhelming

       stench

unlike anything
I've ever experienced.

It's like the walls have been
      slathered with sauerkraut
      soaked with sweat
      simmered in a pot
         with a close-fitting lid.

I gag, cover
my mouth, press
my lips tight.

Gretchen steals a glance
down the corridor before
slipping a key in a jiggly

lock, leading
me through a sitting room that
smells no better than
the corridor and into
a tiny room not much
bigger than a closet containing
nothing more than
a bed, a rickety nightstand.

Nothing
about this place
says

      home.

THE TRUTH OF THE MATTER

I can't help asking

    Is this where you come
    with the men who pay you?

Gretchen sits
on the bed, pats
the space beside
her, a gesture that reminds
me we're alone together
in a bedroom for the

very
first
time.

It's not a bad way
to earn a living, you know.
My days are my own
and I bet we could
even be roommates.

I remain standing
remain flabbergasted
remain unsure
why I even followed
her here.

But before I can express
     my thoughts
     my feelings
     my desire to snatch
        her away from here
the door to the flat opens
heavy footfalls approach
Gretchen jumps
to her feet, grabs
my arms, holds
me in place.

BETRAYED

I struggle
to break free

but

Gretchen only grips
me tighter
while those
footsteps march
        forward

until

a towering man fills
the doorway, crosses
his arms, looks
me up and down.

*Could use some meat on her
but she'll do just fine.*

He nods
at Gretchen, she loosens
her grip

and I tense
        waiting

to see what he'll do
next.

EVEN WORSE

Gretchen slips
past us
out to the sitting room
        leaving
me alone
with this
thick-necked
blond-haired
            monster.

How

                could she

    do this

to me?

THE WORST

He takes
a step closer.

Relax, Liebchen.

I back up
against the wall
shake my head.

I can smell the
garlicky sausage on
his breath
and I don't want
that breath or his
sausage fingers on
my skin

so I listen to
the voice
in my head
                    a voice that sounds
                    like Mutti's

refuse
to subject myself
to this

        stomp

                    on his foot

177

                    knee

him where it matters

                              run

            away.

EMOTIONAL

Tears stream
down my cheeks
        I can't
        catch
        a breath
as my heels hammer
carrying me away

        people staring at the spectacle
                        (me)
                down the entire block.

I can't I can't I can't
                go on
trying to be strong
trying to bravely make
        my way alone

(sniff, sob)

wait.

I stumble
to a stop, suddenly realize
perhaps I don't have to

thinking not of
Gretchen
but of Rosa

because even if
she isn't the girl
I thought she was

even if
a romance doesn't lie
in our future

she's the one person
who's been there
for me since we met

which means

she'll surely be there now
when I need
her most.

THE DOORBELL

I swallow my tears
swallow my fear

hurry through the
familiar streets leading
      toward Rosa
hoping beyond hope
her welcome still stands

         because

I need a warm welcome
now more than ever.

My footsteps echo
right up to the door until
I ring
the bell, shift
in my shoes, wait
for a response.

CRUSHED

I lose
my nerve, shuffle

backward, consider
disappearing

but

when Rosa sees
me, she cries out
my name, frantic
energy seeping
out of her and into
soft red lips that press
        against my cheek
arms that wrap
        around me

        tethering me
                to the ground
                to this girl
                to this home

and

all thoughts of running
away vanish
with my worries.

A RENEWED INVITATION

Rosa clings

    to me

one arm around

    my back, pulls

me inside

    and I let loose

        the torrent of tears

           rushing out of me

    dam burst.

SORRY

We stand there
seconds, minutes
who knows how long

me
    sobbing uncontrollably

Rosa
            holding me
            stroking my hair
            offering comfort

and when I finally slow down
she wipes my tears away, takes
me down the corridor
to the kitchen where
she sits me down, prepares
tea, slices
bread, spreads
it with butter.

My stomach growls and
she finally turns to look
at me, her gaze filled
with hurt feelings.

                        Why didn't you wait for me?
                        Why didn't you come here?
                        She doesn't wait
                                for answers.
                        I was sick with worry.
                        I had no idea where to find you.

She might be hurt now
but I
was hurt then.

It didn't seem like
you'd be looking.

> *I'm so sorry. For that whole night,*
> *truly.*
> *Sorry for the rowdy crowd*
> *that made you stop singing —*
> > *I meant to tell you*
> > *how important it is*
> > *to ignore the audience.*
> *And sorry for that kiss with Lena —*
> > *I certainly didn't think*
> > *what it would mean.*

My chest quivers
as that kiss burns
through my memory
but I'm not about to let
Rosa know how much
it shattered me
    at least not now.

She brings
me a small plate, places
a hand on my arm.

> *I tried to change their minds*
> *tried to assure them of your talent*
> > *tried to save your place.*

Warm hand
    warm heart

apology
accepted.

IDEA EXCHANGE

A few minutes
later, a steaming cup of
tea sits before me, my
bread and butter already
hastily gobbled.

I take a sip, take
a breath, ask
for advice.

> *I don't really know how*
>   *to go about this,*
> I say, my voice sounding
> strangely hollow.
> *But I know I have to try again.*
> *I don't really have a choice.*
> *I need to earn a living.*
> I swallow. *Do you know any*
> *other places I might try singing?*

Do I ever!
Rosa's eyes sparkle.
There are so many fantastic clubs
in Schöneberg
but you simply must try Skorpion-Bar.

Skorpion-Bar?

Named after the novel —
have you read it?
Love between women on the page!
Anyway, the owner of the bar is a gas
and if you do well,
they might ask you to return.
Rosa pauses. *And I know you'll do well.*
Just imagine me sitting there in the
front row.

She lays
a hand on my arm, peering
into my eyes, trapping
my breath in my
throat, freezing
my heart in my
chest.

The clock
on the wall counts
five full seconds

Ticktack
            Ticktack
Ticktack
                Ticktack
    Ticktack

before Rosa withdraws
her hand, resumes
the conversation
        her voice
        a bit
        wobbly.

                            The pianist there is Max.
                            He'll surely get you on the roster
                            if you mention Ute.
                            They're friends.
                            I'll ring and get you
                            on the guest list for Friday.
                            Biggest night of the week!

I'm breathing
again and now I'm
        nodding
agreeing to do this
        wildly
                unlike me
                    thing

as though
everything about me
has suddenly
changed.

APRIL 8, 1932
PREPARATION

A few nights later
equal parts
     anxiety and
     determination
I prepare myself

     or rather

Rosa prepares
me, dusting
powder on my
cheeks, painting
color on my
lips, boosting
my confidence with
her words.

               You are going
               to capture their hearts.
               I only wish
               I could be there
               to hear you.

How I wish
she could be

there
too.

THE IN CROWD

It doesn't take
long to arrive to
Lutherstraße and as soon
as I do, I spot
the Skorpion-Bar
a sign proclaiming

CLOSED FOR PRIVATE PARTY

but Rosa told me to expect
this, to expect
the door closed and
curtains drawn shut
keeping part of
                    Berlin out
and part of
        Berlin in
just like Café Lila.

I slip in the door where
a person in a suit and tie
wearing garish eye makeup

holds a pretty girl in a dress
close
        a girl who checks
        the reservation list
        blows me a kiss
        lets me pass.

Once inside, I'm swallowed by
        flirtatious conversation
        upbeat music
and I make my way to the bar
order a glass of champagne
take in the dance floor
            glowing
under a blinking red traffic light.

This place is no Café Lila
      (because nothing is)
but it certainly has
its charm.

I tip back
my champagne
once, twice, thrice
and when the pianist stops
playing, announces a
break, I muster
courage, imagine Rosa

pulling me along, head
across the floor
toward him.

CONNECTIONS

Others swarm
around the pianist but
it's like something else has
control of my body as
I push forward, elbow my
way to his side, extend
my hand.

> *Max? How do you do?*
> *I'm a friend of Ute's.*

At that precise moment
I realize I know neither
Max's nor Ute's last name

but

lucky for me there's
no one like Ute in
all of Berlin.

You don't say! He lights a cigarette,
leads me away from the crowd.
What can I do for you?

For a brief moment
I ask myself how Rosa or
Lena would present
herself, try
my best to act
like that.

    I'm a singer.
    I'd like to perform.

No tremor in my voice
      no pleading
            no please
no
hesitation.

He takes me in, shakes his head.
Sorry, kid. I'd love to help
but the lineup's full tonight.

POP

My champagne bubbles
    fizzle out

                    broken
as my hopes.

I make my way back
to the bar
order another glass
of champagne
my lipstick left on the rim
the only sign I was here
at all.

TALK ABOUT SPECTACULAR

Max announces a special treat
sharing that the stage
will be graced by

      Claire Waldoff

and I don't know
      what
Rosa was thinking

sending me
to a club
where my idol now stands

performing the same

number from her latest
recording

but I can't help
            watching
transfixed

as she starts
singing, brimming
with heart, with the words

                    Es gibt nur ein Berlin!

the entire
audience
joining along.

ALL OR NOTHING

Claire Waldoff steps
offstage, and
the whole crowd seems

to be holding a
collective breath, waiting
for whatever follows.

I fill myself plump as a

zeppelin, watching Max scan
the crowd, shake his head

    until

he makes eye contact
with me, waves
me forward.

                              Looks like my next act
                              isn't here yet.
                              What's your song, kid?

        "Das Lila Lied."

Fear rises
in my throat, fear I hope
he doesn't detect

and when he nods, I step
into the spotlight like
I belong there.

FOCUS

With the cool metal of the
microphone in my palm, the
faces in the audience blend

                    nothing more than
                        shadows
their bodies shifting
toward me
            an imaginary Rosa shimmering
                    among them
                expectant, enthusiastic.

Once the music runs
from the piano keys through the smoky air
the notes become
part of me
        my breath
        my being.

Cradling the
microphone stand
like a lover, I croon
the first words of the tune
            words everyone here
            surely knows so well
yet no one in the
audience sings along.

I continue
        line after line
sharing this anthem
of my people

different
from the others

and when I finally dare
a glance around the room

drinks sit untouched
      cigarettes untended
groups of friends sit
in rapt attention
forgotten conversations
                hanging
in the air like
tendrils of smoke.

The music
swallows
me whole and
I surrender
to it completely.

My voice
      my song
           myself.

As soon as I finish,
a thunder of
applause crashes
over me and even

Claire Waldoff herself shoots
    surprise
    a raised eyebrow
    a smile
my way and
I feel like an equal

    a star

        a burning light

a singer.

OPEN INVITATION

Max stands
up, slips me
five Reichsmark, invites
me back
anytime.

Not only can
I do
this

I've
done
it.

I float
on air
all the way
back
to Rosa's.

APRIL 9, 1932
EXHAUSTION

Though I try
to stay up for
Rosa, my lack of
sleep the night before makes
my eyelids droop until I give
in and lie on the bed to rest my eyes
and it's daylight by the time I open them again.

SHARING STORIES

Moments after I blink
myself awake, Rosa stirs
at my side
        sighing
        stretching
        shifting
toward me

and how I wish
I could reach out for
her across the invisible
                divide

but her eyelids flutter open like
butterfly wings, revealing

brown eyes deep
as starless night.

I couldn't budge you
when I came home last night.
You fell asleep in your dress!

I look down at
myself in surprise to see
she's right.

Rosa sits up.
Anyway, I tried to wake you
because I have news.
Lena didn't show up
for work last night!

I hear the words but
I don't believe
them.

You should've seen everyone's faces
when I told them you were singing
at Skorpion-Bar. She grips my arm.
You did perform there, didn't you?

I nod.

How did it go? Tell me everything!

It went
swimmingly.

Swimmingly?

Swimmingly.

Rosa squeals, wraps
her arms around my
shoulders.

> *I knew it. I knew it!*
> *But you have to come back*
> *to us now, to Café Lila.*
> *I didn't even have to suggest it.*
> *Emil brought it up.*

Emil? I blink.
Perhaps he doesn't completely
dislike me after all.

Max's offer to return
and perform again
at Skorpion-Bar beckons
like forbidden gold

but

Café Lila plants

itself in my mind the same
way it's planted
itself in my
heart and there's only
one answer I can give.

Jawohl!

ACHES AND PAINS

As the day wears
on, my head begins to

thrum

then throb

then pound

the initial ache deepening
into full-blown agony.

Evidently the buildup
from losing

everything

and gaining

it back

is too much so
I'm headed
to the pharmacist.

COLLISION

I pay for my purchase, slip
the bottle into my pocket, exit
back to the street

where I crash
into someone in a hurry just
outside the shop.

Lena.

What are you doing here?
She snarls as though I have no
right to be here
at a public pharmacy.

She pushes
past me, and I pause
unable to bring
myself to leave
while she's in such

obvious distress and
while guilt floods me that
    what was once hers
        will soon be mine.

Moments later, she bursts
back outside, stutters
to a stop beside me, sighs.

        What? Did you wait for me
        so you could gloat?
        Lena crosses her arms.

    Gloat? Nein. I shake
    my head. *I —*

        I'll make it easy for you all
        and your gossip.
        My little sister Lottchen's sick.
        I couldn't leave her alone last night.
        This medicine is her last hope.

She squeezes
a bottle of pills in
her fist, daring
it to defy her, glaring
at me like it's my fault.

I hold a hand to my chest.

I'm so sorry, I say.
I hope she pulls through.

Lena's narrowed eyes soften.
Danke.

We look at each other in
awkward silence for
another moment
　　a moment when I remember
　　Gretchen and how she treated me

　　　　before I remember
　　　　　　　　Rosa
　　　　and her
　　　　kindness

and I decide that even though
Lena only looks out for
herself and people like her

I want to be
　　like Rosa
not Gretchen

so I ask

What do you need?
I mean, other than the medicine.

                    Lena doesn't hesitate. *Money.*
                    I need money.

Once again my mouth blurts
out words before I think
them through
        Let's split it.

Lena gives me
a blank look in response
and I know I have to explain.

        Emil offered me the job
        after you didn't show up
        and I'm definitely taking it —
        I need the money too.
                    But . . .
        if we split the job, split the pay
        at least we'll both get something.

                    Lena narrows her eyes
                    crosses her arms. *Fine.*
                    When my sister's feeling better
                            I'll be there.

Time will tell
if my offer was brilliant
                or foolhardy.

REST, RELEASE, READY

I return
to Rosa's, kick
off my shoes, take
my medicine.

She has me rest
on the settee, makes
me feel at home and I'm
            out
within minutes, gone.

When a hand gently jostles
my shoulder, I drag
my eyelids open to find
the room's gone dark
the day disappeared.

                Feeling better? Rosa's voice
                is as gentle as her hand.

I nod, slowly sit
up, rub

my eyes, get
ready to return to

    Café Lila.

REALITY

After spending the past few days
    entrenched
in my own problems

passing the column on the corner
plastered with politics
      reminds
me there's more going on
in the world.

      ENOUGH WITH

    HITLER'S SEDITION!

    VOTE HINDENBURG!

      HITLER!

    THE FAITH AND HOPE

        OF MILLIONS!

    CAPITALISM IS STEALING

    YOUR LAST PIECE OF BREAD!

    VOTE THÄLMANN!

I grab Rosa's arm.
          The runoff election!
          I completely forgot.
          When is it again?

                              Tomorrow. Rosa grimaces.
                              Hopefully everything will go
                              back to normal after it's over.

I hope she's right
          but
if it's anything like
the last election
I have my doubts.

CAFÉ LILA

Almost as soon as we arrive
Rosa's already switched
her attention from politics
to me.

                              Look! I've got Hilde,
                              fresh after her debut
                              on the Skorpion-Bar stage!

Brigitte raises
an eyebrow, looks

to me for confirmation
    but
Ute isn't so patient.

        So it's really true?

    That I sang
    at Skorpion-Bar?
    I did.

        And it went swimmingly.
        Rosa grins, puffed up with pride.

        If you'd finished your song
        last week, Brigitte grumbles,
        you might have kept your job.

        Maybe tonight's her lucky
        night! Ute says.
        Let's see what she can do.

REHEARSAL

Ute asks
what I sang
last night, asks
for a repeat.

I step
to the microphone and
though the only
people watching are
       Ute
       Brigitte
       Rosa

I feel their eyes
on me, their ears
perked up and
the pressure's on as
I begin "Das Lila Lied."

The best thing I can do
is block them out, so I do,
imagining the thick haze of
smoke and dim club lights
              obscuring
everything beyond
the stage
until it's only

the microphone and me

and I sing, crooning
the words I know
so well, words
that have made their

way into my heart, words
that define me and
everyone in this club

different
from the others

and when I finish
the reaction is
immediate
overwhelming.

Rosa squeals, Brigitte claps,
Ute calls, *Bravo!*

*Who knew we had such a talent
in our midst?* Brigitte smiles.

Rosa flounces
toward me, wraps
an arm around my
shoulders.

*There's nothing as lovely
as your voice, Liebchen.*

And I don't think I could
possibly
soar higher.

APRIL 10, 1932
ENSEMBLE

The next day is
election day
and we're all
      preoccupied

so as we prepare to go on
at the club that evening
it seems like the perfect
moment to share
the news that escapes
my mouth.

    I meant to tell you all
    something.

        Brigitte stops,
        leans over the bar.
        I'm listening.

Rosa raises
an eyebrow.

    I ran into Lena yesterday.
    Her little sister's been sick but
    I asked her to come back here
    once she's feeling better.

Brigitte sighs. *We've been over*
this before. We can't keep both of
you.

A door slams.

We think you can.
Lena approaches.
Hilde and I made a deal.
We're prepared
          to split the job and
                    the pay —
          at least for now.

She meets my gaze
daring me to say
otherwise.

Brigitte pauses, then nods.
Well, if you put it that way
fine by me.

But Lena's not done yet.
And if we bring in
          more of a crowd with
          more of us onstage
surely you'll pay us what we're
worth.

Brigitte raises an eyebrow.
We'll have to see about that.

MORE REHEARSAL

We're running
out of time, but we have
just enough to practice
a new song together
            the one Claire Waldoff sang
                    about Berlin
the perfect number
for us to animate
the audience while the city
tallies today's votes.

All of us are familiar with
the runaway hit and it's
easy to divide up the lines
between the three of us.
Ute of course plays the tune
as effortlessly as any other
so soon enough we are
                    ready
to wow the crowd with
a performance
        unlike any

done here
before.

FILLING UP

The club fills
    the tables fill
        the air fills

with
    laughter
    conversation
    joy buzzing

        through
            and through

me and
Rosa and
Lena and
the Vogel sisters and
Katja and Käthe and
the rest of the crowd
the electric environment evident
when Emil and Erich arrive.

Ute stubs
out a cigarette, nods

to the three of
us and we head
backstage, prepare
to go on.

ES GIBT NUR EIN BERLIN

Rosa steps
onstage first

and although my
heartbeat thunders
in my
      chest
      head
      ears

I trick
myself into exuding
confidence as I follow
          ready
to perform this
snappy number
          ready
to do my part to ensure
we have the jobs
and the pay we all so
desperately need.

Rosa and I begin
standing arm in arm
in front of
the microphone, celebrating
our magical city.

Rosa waves
Lena forward, inviting
her onstage and we
        surround
her, one of us at
each elbow.

                                        Lena jumps right in,
                                        hand to her chest, singing
                                        Es gibt nur ein Berlin.

I bend toward
the microphone, sing
the next line, sure
of my voice as I am
        of anything.

The audience erupts
in cheers
and we're bundled
up in it with them

            floating

on the sensation of
this shared bliss
for the city we love
as much as life itself.

SCOUTING

Once the song ends we attempt
to keep the crowd animated
about the Berlin we all still adore.

Rosa and Lena stand
behind me to sing
            backup
as I launch
into "Das Lila Lied"
and I'm thrilled
to hear everyone join
in on the refrain
even more thrilled
as they settle down to listen.

When I finish to
resounding applause, I step out
of the spotlight, see
a slim man in a
smart suit standing

at Ute's side thrusting
a card forward.

A cigarette
        dangles
from his mouth, his
bowler hat low over
his eyes, but he tips
it up for a look at me.

Before I decide
if I should cross
the stage, he's gone,
his figure vanishing
into the thick smoke.

                Ute holds up the card.
                Artiphon-Record!
                A thumbs-up.

                    Rosa squeals.
                    He was from a record label!
                    Well done, Hilde!

Even Lena gives
me a curt nod of
        approval
                alongside a dash of
                barely concealed envy.

A record label!

This is
        more
than I ever
expected.

STANDING OVATION

More songs
more service
more of a whirlwind

as we return
to the floor with
trays of drinks that
the most joyful patrons
seem pleased to share
with me

and soon enough we're
back onstage for
our final set singing
"Es gibt nur ein Berlin"
to even more enthusiasm
than before, but
suddenly it's clear that
not all the faces in

the audience are
friendly.

I freeze.
The man who was
at the rally with Lena, the
man Emil had called
                    a war veteran,
is the man now marching
toward the stage, stopping only
to point a gnarly finger at
Lena.

I was right! Immoral whore!
Performing in a nightclub
with these tramps!
Adolf Hitler and his party
will put an end to places like this
after they win!

Conversation ceases
around the tables
            until
Emil gets to his feet
barrels his way over
to Lena's father, points
a finger at his chest.

Raus! This is my club
and I don't want to see
you or your men here
ever again.

Jaws clenched, eyes narrowed
Lena's father shrugs away
from Emil's finger, nods
at his companions, thrusts
himself back toward the door.

Lena stares
cheeks white as chalk
before jumping
off the stage and
        hurtling
after him.

APRIL 11, 1932
HEADLINES

The next morning, I awake
slowly

> the blur of performances at Café Lila
> the man from the record label
> Lena's father's sudden appearance
> > all racing through my mind

and I burrow
under the sheets, savor
this luxurious life, knowing
it could disappear
in an instant.

Tante Esther is
already up, clattering
in the kitchen, frying
what smells like potatoes.

And then I remember
the most important
thing.

> *The vote!*

> > Rosa pops to sitting.

Tante Esther will have
the paper.

She hops out of bed,
leads the way to
the kitchen.

I wordlessly roll
out of bed, rush
after her.

Guten Morgen.
Tante Esther smiles.

A good sign.
Who won?

We slip
onto our seats, our
places already set, this
lovely kitchen, this
entire flat brimming
with home.

Tante Esther sits
across from us, picks
up the *Vossische Zeitung*,
points to the headline.

Hindenburg, she says. *That old goat.*
At least he's a devil we know.

Rosa and I let
out breaths of
relief.

But Adolf Hitler still did well.
Over thirteen million votes!
Why don't people see
what he stands for?

At least it's over, Rosa says.

For now, Tante Esther says.
But times are getting tougher.

She clears
her throat, tension crackles
through the air.

You know, my mother
left me a nice savings.
Your Bubbe. She nods at Rosa.
But I didn't expect to need it
so soon.

What are you saying?
Rosa sits up straighter.

It's nothing to worry about
too much yet.
I was let go from the office.
          I'm a statistic.
One of six million unemployed.
Could each of you spare
a few Reichsmark a week for the rent?

I glance at Rosa, speak
for us both.

          Of course.
          Whatever it takes.

But Rosa's eyes grow
large in her pale face,
like the dark and
icy fear I've known
most of my life has
finally struck
her for the
very
first
time.

This, after I just agreed
to do my job for half
the pay.

I decide

    then

               and
      there

to find a way to earn
some extra income that
will make a real
difference to this
household, to this
    home.

POSSIBILITIES

After breakfast, I rush
to get ready, plans bubbling
up in my head as quickly as
I can prepare myself.

I fasten on
a lush set of eyelashes, paint
my lips a shimmering red, peer
in the mirror.
I look older
    dangerous.

Rosa flops on the bed.
Where are you off to?

After everything Tante Esther
has done for me
I have to do something
        else
find a way to contribute
            more.

Rosa raises
an eyebrow
and I want nothing more
than to say
how much I want
to please her
but I can't risk sharing
feelings like those.

    I'll be back
    before work.

ON MY WAY

Once I'm out the door, I pull
the card from my pocketbook.
The embossed letters read

HERMANN EISNER

BEUTHSTRASSE 1

KREUZBERG BERLIN

I head
for the Hoch-und Untergrundbahn
for the trip across the city.

At Wittenbergplatz, I climb
down the stairs, wait
on the platform with
a handful of others

> an older gentleman, puffing on a pipe
> a couple of young men in caps pacing
> a woman giving me a disapproving glance.

Perhaps my makeup is
too much for daylight.

But the train roars
in the station and I thrill
at the idea of traveling
through the city to meet
the executive of a record label.

I step aboard, settle
in as the train snakes
its way east through the

crowds at Potsdamer Platz to
my stop, Spittelmarkt.

But once I step
out to the street, I realize
I should've planned better.
I've never been to
this part of Kreuzberg.

Excuse me. I approach
a round-faced middle-aged man.

> *Can you direct me
> toward Beuthstraße?*

> *That way.* He points, steps closer,
> his expression twisting.
> *Unless you'd rather come with me.*
> He jangles a pocketful of coins.

It's just like
Gretchen's all over again.

> *Nein!*

I choke
out the word, speed
away.

THE RECORDING STUDIO

After my escape
I wander
     lost
finally find Beuthstraße,
the building I seek, march
inside.

A glance at
the directory, a jaunt down
the hallway, and there it stands
     my future
     painted right on
     the glass

    ARTIPHON-RECORD

I pull myself straighter, take
a deep breath, knock.

               Herein! A deep voice
               commands me to enter.

I'm here to see
Herr Eisner.

               Well, indeed you are.
               The man at the desk winks.

He takes a puff on a stinky cigar,
pushes himself to standing.
Come with me.

I take stock of the
narrow corridor, the lack of

protection
friendly faces
escape.

But this is for my career.

Even more, this is for Rosa.

I follow
the man to another door to
a dimly lit room, where
the man from the club stands
                    hovering
over some recording equipment.

A pretty young thing for you.

Ach so! Herr Eisner looks up,
eyebrows raised.
*Good to see you
so soon.*

I awkwardly shake
his hand, try
to relax.

You may leave us, Rudi.
Herr Eisner waves,
the man shuffles off.
Remind me of your name.

The walls seem to edge
in a bit closer. Hildegard.
Hilde.

Well, Hilde, I've been trying
to get this equipment to work.
Why don't you warm up
and then we can give it a go?

All right. I set
my pocketbook on the table, run
through some scales, a few bars of
"Das Lila Lied" and
        focus, focus, focus
before I give
Herr Eisner a nod.

Here we go. He wraps an arm
around my waist, draws me in front
of the microphone. Now!

236

I move
ever so slightly away
from his touch, launch
into "Das Lila Lied," let
my voice ring
clear in the closed-in space.

Everything slips
from my mind.

I sing

        and sing

    and sing

and when I finish

    clicks and whirs sound

from the machine

I step
away

take
a breath

wait.

THE GLORY OF HOPE

I don't have
to wait long.

> *I've got it!*
> Herr Eisner's voice pops
> with excitement.

He places
the needle on the record
a crackle bursts
through the speaker
a lush, velvety voice
sings.

> *Is that really me?*
> I hold a hand to my chest.

> *It is indeed.* He grins.
> *Some girls sing fine*
> *in the clubs, freeze up here.*
> *Not you. You've got real talent.*

Talent! A shot of
confidence surges
through me.

> *Why don't you come back*

in a few weeks? He pauses.
What you'll really need
is some original material.
Got anything?

Certainly, I fib.
Coming up with
new songs can't
be all that hard.

And a pianist. He gestures to
the piano against the wall.
Unless you play?

I shake my head.

Well, just bring someone along.
And here you go.
He picks the disc up,
slips it in paper, hands it to me.
Consider this a gift.

Danke. I breathe.
Auf Wiedersehen.

My thoughts swimming
with hope, I stride
down the hall and into
the dazzling

brightness
of day.

NEXT STEPS

I clutch
the recording to my chest, hurry
back toward the train,
everything around me
just as it was before

       shoppers off to market
       rumbles of vehicles
       the promise of fresh
            spring air

yet so much has
changed.

I have talent, confirmed
by a record executive!

I never trusted
myself to believe
I might actually have
a future as a
professional
singer

               just
               like
               Mutti
one who might even earn
a living from it
but the paper cover crinkles
in my hands
          all the proof I need
and I can't wait
to share it
with Rosa.

ROUND TRIP

My heels clack
down the stairs to the
station, and I pace, waiting
for the next train.

I imagine telling
everyone at the club about
the recording
          Ute, Brigitte, Emil, even Lena.

Then I remember
Lena's father and
her flight from
the club and

her little sister
at home and
guilt floods
me.

I wonder
what happened
when they got
home.

Another train clunks
over the tracks, coming
to a halt in the station.

I step inside
    freeze
        stare.

The car's filled
with young men my
age or even younger, all wearing
short pants and shirts the
same shade of brown as
the SA soldiers.

One of them jumps
to his feet, offers
me his seat.

I nod
my thanks, slip
into the seat, try to make
myself small
amidst all this
maleness.

When's it starting?

One o'clock.
We should be right on time.

More boys load
the car at each stop
all of them evidently headed
to some kind of Nazi rally.

I squirm in my seat.

As triumphant as my
session with Herr Eisner was,
I can't escape
the world around
me

including the thirteen million
people who voted
for Adolf Hitler

and what else they might
be planning.

When the young men brush
past me out the car at
Leipziger Platz, I

hesitate

but only for a moment
before I'm compelled
to follow.

FOLLOWER

The station's crammed
with a horde of
brown-shirted boys
        heading
to the street.

I hang
behind the group, wait
for the crowd to
                dissipate.

I consider
        turning back

to catch the next train,
but this situation
    all these Hitler supporters
        gathered here
    so soon after the election
is anything
but ordinary

and someone
has to see
it, share
it, do
something.

WOLF PACK

I step into
the sunlight, lower
my cloche over my eyes, but
the impossible crowd has swelled.

Clumps of boys
signs proclaiming
    HITLER YOUTH

    THE JEWS ARE OUR MISFORTUNE

Across the square, the Wertheim
department store gleams,

its windows marred only by the
reflection of those
ugly signs outside.

I have no desire
to be here for this and
I promise myself
I can leave
in a few minutes but
someone must witness
the scope of this
        our clear enemy.

A platform at the
end of the block

        an imposing man in
        a brown uniform stepping
        forward to speak

            the entire street of
            boys pushing
            forward with
            new energy.

                        It's Herr von Schirach!
                        The party's youth chief!

The frenzy that sets

over these boys turns
them into wild animals, but
when the man begins to speak,
a hush falls
over the square.

I watch, listen.

Through loudspeakers, his
message rings
out over the spellbound
public
            not admitting the defeat
                    of the election
            instead calling to fight
            against the dangers of Bolshevism
                    and
            for the return of Germany's
                    glory and pride
            through faith in the promise
            of its youth.

He finishes his speech, departs,
and the audience explodes
            arms rise
cheers sound
            the boys surge
in a monstrous wave as
another speaker approaches,

spends several long minutes
ranting about Jews
being the root
of all that's wrong
with Germany

        making me think of
        Rosa and Tante Esther and
        how this couldn't be further from
                the truth
        how they've been nothing but kind
                to me

so a glance
over the crowd is
all I need

to know
who
the real villains are.

WEHRT EUCH!

Nazi signs warn
Germans

        DEFEND YOURSELVES!
        DON'T BUY FROM JEWS!

but I decide I must
defend myself

not against Jewish people
but against

      people

         like these.

THE NEXT TARGET

Once the speakers finish
the stage empties
the square rises in cheers
the crowd begins to disperse
but another influx of bodies shoots
out from a side street
near me.

             No more immorality!

Veterans wearing uniforms
from the Great War shuffle
forward, chests puffed proud
as the crowd makes way
for their approach.

Where is he?
Where's Braun?

A man surges forward, pushing
against the backs of
those in his way.

Lena's father.

Shut down the queer nightclubs!

He marches ahead
while his friends clap
him on the back, swallowing
him and the others like a pack of
wolves.

CALM IN THE STORM

The official speeches now over
Lena's father makes his way
to the stage
his words reaching
the smaller crowd with
a surprising calm.

My good young men

Berliner
Deutscher.
The time has come to fight
the immorality worming
through our city.
I ask you to stand with us, to do
what is right, moral, good.
Help us shut down the clubs,
drive these queer degenerates
from Berlin
by any means necessary!

Thunderous applause rises
again, swallowing
every bit of kindness in
the city.

My breath chokes
in my throat.

They want to attack
not only Jewish people
but also people like me
      meaning people like Rosa
      are doubly in danger.

I've seen
enough.

Pushing my way through
the crowd, I hurry
through the streets taking
great gulps of air.

The more space I put
between me
and this rally,
the better.

PREPARATIONS

By the time I make
it back, the sky has
clouded over, there's
not much time to talk

and Rosa's busy
readying herself for
the night ahead

      so

I set the recording
aside, freshen up as
competing thoughts of
     good news
          and

        somber news
chase themselves
around my head

until

Rosa pushes
herself to her feet, gives
me a dejected look

        one that nearly crushes
                my heart

                filling my mind with worry
                making me wonder
                        if I did something wrong

but instead of explaining
she only asks
if I'm ready to go.

WRONGDOING

I follow
Rosa out the door
down to the street
now glistening with
raindrops

my mind whirring
        all the while

I finally catch
up, wake
up, place
a hand on
Rosa's arm.

      Is everything all right?

Rosa comes
to a
      dead
      halt
right there on the sidewalk
shakes her head
says nothing.

I frown, swallow, decide
on distraction.

      Shall I tell you
      what happened to me today?

Rosa nods, resumes
her march forward
and

I spill
everything

    the good and
    the bad

hoping the spilling
will brighten
her mood

hoping
my efforts
are enough.

THIS GIRL

Once I share
Rosa relaxes, reacting
in all the right places

    pleased as I am
    about the recording
           excited
       to hear it herself

shocked as I am
about the rally

though I keep
the more frightening details
        to myself

but

when I ask her again

        Is everything all right?

she looks at me and
I am a useless
melted
        mess
of a girl
                but

she takes
my hand in hers
and with

        one
        soft
        squeeze

there's room
in my heart

for no one and
        nothing

but
her.

APRIL 14, 1932
STILL, THIS GIRL

It goes on like this
all week
Rosa keeping
to herself, keeping
quiet

until Thursday evening
on the way to the club
in a soft rain
I gather
courage, ask
in a whisper

   Please tell me what's going on.

Rosa's face flashes
with secret dark thoughts

   and

she opens her mouth
talking barely
over a whisper.

     It's my home, my life, my family.
     I've taken Tante Esther for

granted all along
assumed everything would be fine
and now that it might not be
now that she's lost her job
who knows what will be next?
Tears well up in her eyes.
I can't bear to lose anything else.
The hole inside me
the one my parents left
is already eating me alive.

With these words
I realize that
even the most loving
aunt isn't enough

that Rosa and I
are more alike than
I ever imagined.

MEMORY

My first night

at the orphanage

I felt like

someone had scooped

my insides out

hollowing me

like a rotting log.

COMPARING NOTES

I blurt out
my own truth.

> *Losing your parents*
> *is the hardest thing*
> *in the world.*

The clouds and
the sky take this moment
to unleash a torrent
of heavier rain and
Rosa has to raise
her voice to be heard.

> *Some things are even harder.*
> *Like your parents leaving you*
> *for drugs.*

Morphine
killed my parents.

Tears stream
down Rosa's face
like the deluge
down the street.

I thought life with Tante Esther
would be stable
would be forever.
I lost my home
            my family
            once.
I can't let it happen
                    again.

Nothing I say
can heal that
hurt, that
fear

so I step closer
she steps closer
            and something new
                    shines through
            her eyes
the way she's taking in
                    my lips

but

she's so
                    vulnerable

what she needs
is a friend

so

         my arms wrap
                    around her

                    and hers wrap
         around me

and all I want is
to forget the past

                    mine
         and
                    hers

and to freeze
                    this moment
in time.

A NEW PARTNERSHIP

By the time we arrive
at Café Lila, the rain's slowed
to a drizzle.

Rosa and I share
a secret smile
as she sets her umbrella
in the stand, hangs
up her hat, and I give
her arm one more squeeze
before approaching Ute at the bar.

Ute, can I ask you something?

Fire away!

I went to Artiphon-Record the other day —

And?

And it went wonderfully but —

Ute raises an eyebrow
waiting.

*He wants me to come back with
some original material*

                    and
              a pianist.

I wince, afraid
my request is too forward.

                              Happy to help with both!
                              Ute beams, steps over to the piano.
                              What do you have in mind?

I bend
close, whisper
my ideas, even hum
a few bars of a
melody

and

we get right to
work, Ute picking
up my melody, improvising
along with it, improving
my original tune until
what's coming off
the keys sounds
        less
like dabbling and
        more

like the beginnings of
a real song

        and

we still have lots of work
ahead of us but I'm flying
high as high can be
by the time Brigitte opens
the doors, lets
the crowd in.

ESPIONAGE

Lena arrives even later than usual
        breathless
        her cloche low over her eyes
and she wordlessly heads
past the full tables toward
backstage not even saying hello
                to Emil
returned to the club for the first time
since last week.

He shares a suspicious look
with Brigitte, waves
me over to the bar.

I approach with cautious steps.

Say, see if you can find out
if our pal Lena's on the up-and-up.

I raise an eyebrow
not trusting myself to say
anything this time.

Look, she's from the neighborhood and
I wanted to help her out but
I don't want her attracting
that kind of crowd in here again,
putting us in danger. He straightens
   his tie.
I know you felt bad for her too
with her sick little sister and all but
we might be better off without her.

Anyway, let me know what you learn.
I promise I'll listen this time.
We all trust you, Hilde.

With these last words
I realize not only
Brigitte but also Ute
are listening in, nodding
their approval

and my heart swells
          with love
for this place and
these people.

I press
my lips together, nod
to all of them, scurry
backstage.

SPILLED SECRETS

Lena's peering at herself
in the vanity mirror
adjusting her cloche

when Rosa approaches
playfully tips
it off her head

          only to reveal a
          swollen dark bruise
          on Lena's cheek.

                    Give me that!
                    Lena snatches her hat back
                    sets it on her head, winces.

Rosa hesitates.
Was it your father?

Almost unbelievably
this handful of words
spoken so kindly

break this tough girl
            down
into tears

and none of us says anything
more as the three of us
softly embrace

just three girls
understanding
one another.

REPORTING

After our first performance
of the evening I make
the rounds with
tray after tray of drinks

making sure to stop at Emil's table
            unintentionally interrupting

the passionate kiss
he's sharing with Erich

to leave them two fresh
glasses of champagne along
with the news that Lena couldn't
                    possibly support

a man
like
her
father

that she's
indeed
on the
up-and-up

that she
should
definitely
stay.

APRIL 15, 1932
DREAMY

The next day it's back
to the routine that includes

      working with Ute on our song
      along with a few other new tunes
            in their infancy

and this isn't going to be as quick
         as I thought
but collaborating with someone
who understands
how to blend
the right words with
the right notes

has me floating
on the thrill of
this music, letting
my voice cement
me here, my home away
from home.

Ute's cheery smile brightens
the entire room

Brigitte stands
at the bar mesmerized

        Rosa steps
        closer

even Lena stops
cleaning to listen

and my voice rings
over us all
    singing
this partially written piece with
real words I've scribbled down
    Shining faces
    take me places
mixed with placeholders
        la, la, la
all to Ute's jaunty tune.

        Wunderbar! Brigitte applauds.

I stumble
over my own feet, try to pull
myself together.

        Rosa beams.
        You're a dream, Hilde.

My cheeks burn.
It's a team effort.
I gesture to Ute who waves
off the praise.

Rosa takes
my hand, her sparkling eyes
making me want to get
closer and closer
until there's no space
between us
at all.

BIG NEWS

It's almost time
to open the doors when
Emil and Erich burst in
followed by Kurt
eyes shifting, lanky body bouncing
(always so nervous
that boy).

But Emil smiles
around the room, steals
the spotlight.

Have you heard the news?
Chancellor Brüning banned the SA!

How'd he manage that? Ute
asks.

Good old Article 48!

Both the president and the chancellor
have been ruling by decree for years
using Article 48 of the constitution

(the only article I know)

to declare
a national emergency

but this time it's perfect
because I can already tell
a ban like this will make us feel
safer on the streets.
No more Brownshirts!

A cheer bursts
from my mouth
from Rosa's mouth
around the room

and we're all so elated
about this greatest
news that it seems
we can do anything
together.

PAYDAY

At the end of the night
Brigitte calls us over
reminding me
it's Friday.

She counts out
thirty Reichsmark
for Rosa as usual
and as Lena and I wait
for our fifteen Reichsmark each
Brigitte's hand hovers
over the till
her mouth twitching
forehead wrinkling
until she slowly counts out
five extra Reichsmark each.

*Having the three of you
has been drawing a bigger crowd,*
she says. *Keep it up and*

we'll see if we can get you both
back up to full pay.

Lena nods and thanks her
    all businesslike
before disappearing with Kurt   .

but I can't help myself
and before I know it
I'm leaning over the bar

giving Brigitte a hug
because I know this is about
more than the bigger crowd

this is her big heart
taking care of us
like family.

May 1932

MAY 14, 1932
NOT REALLY A SURPRISE

Several weeks later
on our way to work
Rosa and I round the last corner
and nearly stumble
into a couple
           their eyes shut
           bodies pressed close
           lost to the world
snapping out of their embrace
only with our near miss

           Lena and Kurt.

They step apart, straighten
their clothing, look
embarrassed

but

I for one am pleased for her
that she might have found
a hint of happiness

and

a shared glance with Rosa
reveals she's thinking
exactly the same thing.

FRIENDSHIP

Kurt scurries off and
Rosa and I waggle
our eyebrows, corner
Lena for the details.

Well, Rosa says, her pretty mouth
a round O.

Lena frowns, crosses
her arms, but
can only manage
to hold the façade for
a few seconds before
breaking down.

All right, all right.
You caught us fair and square.
She leans in close.
I'm hoping Kurt will be
my ticket out of here.

Out of where?
Café Lila?
I ask.

Maybe. She shrugs.
I don't really mind it here
as much as I thought.
                She frowns
as though thinking of
something else.
But no. I aim to leave home
as soon as I can. And I'm
taking Lottchen with me.
All I need is a ring on my finger.

I don't blame her
in the slightest.
In fact if I were her
I'd do whatever I could
to get out of that
situation too.

Well, we wish you all the best,
don't we, Hilde? Rosa says.

Indeed.

The three of us lock arms,
proceed inside Café Lila
our feet fairly skipping

though I admit to myself
I'm hoping to find
luck in love too.

MAY 30, 1932
MORNING NEWS

Despite good things
happening around us
political tensions continue
to mount over the next
couple of weeks with
the news from up top
hardly pointing to a
rosy future.

In fact, by the end
of the month it's
                another day
another disastrous headline

    BRÜNING'S CABINET RESIGNS

    PRESIDENT HINDENBURG ACCEPTS

    THE CHANCELLOR'S RESIGNATION

Tante Esther shakes
her head at the news
explaining how Brüning

    though known as the
    hunger chancellor
        for his years in charge

while unemployment crept
upward

was actually one of the last leaders
trying to uphold the republic

*Without his efforts
to hold it together,* she says,
*the extremes will likely
take hold.*

The three of us
share a somber glance
hopes shattered.

AFTERNOON NEWS

The very same day
the afternoon newspaper
reports

HINDENBURG RECEIVES

HITLER AND GÖRING

FOR LONGER DISCUSSIONS

and it appears
Tante Esther was right
about the extremes if

Hindenburg is looking
to the Nazis
for support.

MAY 31, 1932
MORNING NEWS

Already the next morning the
headline blares another
new announcement

> FRANZ VON PAPEN WILL BE CHANCELLOR
>
> OF A GOVERNMENT WITH A "NATIONAL CONCENTRATION"
>
> DISSOLUTION OF THE REICHSTAG PROBABLE

> *A "national concentration"?*
> *That's not good. Not good at all.*
> Tante Esther shakes her head.

Rosa and I share a glance

    we know "national"

        means

    Nazis

and without a word
both of us spiral away
into a whirlwind of worry.

DISTRACTION

We dress
    slowly
    methodically
    silently
until Rosa stamps
her foot, chasing
our doom out the door.

        We can't do anything about
        the chaos in the government
        and we don't have to work
            until tonight.
        How would you feel about
        getting away for the day?
        Her eyes sparkle.

As usual, I find it
    impossible
to say no to Rosa
but
we're supposed to be
frugal with our finances.

      As long as it doesn't cost much.
      What do you have in mind?

We'll go to Wannsee.
The train fare is cheap and
it's early in the season
so it won't be crowded.
Again, a mischievous glint
in her eyes.

Why not?

I return Rosa's smile
prepare for a respite
from reality.

ESCAPE

We head
out to Wannsee
for sun and sand and cool water
before all the crowds of summer arrive.

It's beautiful but
best of all
are those little
looks
touches
moments
of *almost*
between us.

I don't suppose
I've ever
        felt
so carefree.

There's nowhere
in this world
I'd rather be.

RETURN

When the sun begins
to dip in the sky
Rosa takes
me by the hand, pulls
me to my feet

        her fingers lingering
                on my skin

when I stand over her
blocking the sun.

I so badly want to grab
my impulse and
lean forward
toward her

in what could be
the perfect moment

but I can't ruin
what we have
      can't ruin
            this

so instead
of closing the distance
between us

I bite my lip,
turn
away.

June 1932

JUNE 3, 1932
SELF-CONTROL

After the glorious day at
the lake with Rosa

the only thought running
through my head

for days (and nights) afterward
is how hard it was

sitting there on the sand next to
her

getting my feet wet with
        her

being so close to
                her

and not kissing
her.

SECRET SONGWRITING

I realize that someday
I'm going to have to tell

Rosa how I feel
so on Friday I grab
my notebook and pencil
head out to the nearby
park at Savignyplatz
settle on a bench.

Sitting there listening to
birdsong, I finally let
my feelings pour out
from my pencil
drafting the first lines
of a song not only for
a potential record contract

but more important

a song
        for her.

JUNE 4, 1932
NEW MONTH, NEW CHAOS

Just days after
Papen
is named chancellor
the *Vossische Zeitung* blasts
a new headline

GOVERNMENT DECLARATION

REICHSTAG DISSOLUTION ORDERED

NEW EMERGENCY DECREE ENACTED

and like that
new Reichstag elections are
announced
        for July 31
which means Berlin
will be blanketed with
    campaigns
    slogans
    rallies
from all the political parties
vying for seats

for close to
two
months

and I don't know
how much more chaos
this city can take.

MORE NEWS

The disarray of
the government would
be bad enough and
indeed Rosa and I fidget
over the headline alone

but as Tante Esther reads
on, sharing
bits and pieces from
the *Vossische Zeitung,*

she comes across another
piece of news buried
on the next page.

More trouble. She presses her lips
together.
*Adolf Hitler has requested Papen
to lift the ban on the SA.*

Can he do that? Rosa blinks.

I'm afraid it's looking like
he can do anything.

Even though it hasn't happened
yet, I can already sense
Brownshirts patrolling
the streets again

      greater in number
             and
      madder than wasps.

REDIRECTION

I step away
from the newspaper, step away
from this cycle of disaster after disaster

launch myself
back into the scribbled
lines in my notebook

edit, move, erase
words until I decide
what my words really need is music

which means I need to figure out

a surreptitious way
to share this song with Ute.

KINDERLEICHT

In the end it's easier
than expected to slip
my note in front of the
sheet of music
urging Ute to keep
these lyrics a secret
from Rosa, from everyone

and though Ute's grins are
usually some of the brightest
        at Café Lila
this particular grin outshines
them all.

A nod of the head
a scribbled note back to me
a promise to meet here
once a week
an hour before
everyone else arrives
to work together to make
this song shine.

JUNE 15, 1932
AFTERNOON NEWS

Over a week later
Rosa and I are listening
to records in the sitting room
when Tante Esther returns
home, her expression bursting
with surprise.

> *I've got good news and bad,*
> she says.

> *Bitte, start with the good,*
> Rosa begs.

> *All right.* Tante Esther smiles.
> *I've got a job interview tomorrow!*
> *As a stenographer at Ullstein Verlag.*

We squeal our
congratulations, mirror
Tante Esther's smile
with our own

but

the bad news hangs
over us, making our smiles

fade away prematurely
when she pulls the
evening *Vossische Zeitung*
from under her arm, reads
the headline.

PARTY UNIFORMS AGAIN

REICH DECREE SIGNED

IN SPITE OF PROTESTS

THE SA IS BACK AFTER FRIDAY

and that's it
we've lost
the freedom
we so briefly
enjoyed.

July 1932

JULY 24, 1932
LOOMING DOOM

Tante Esther didn't
get the job

    the SA are back on the
    streets in full force

        with fights breaking out
           between
        Nazis and Communists
        all over Berlin

    and week after week passes by
    with no good news in sight.

One Sunday morning
with the Reichstag elections
just a week away
I'm feeling helpless and
hopeless, lounging beside
Rosa on the settee
the two of us strewn there
like broken pieces of clockwork.

        I'm going to canvass
        for the Social Democrats today.

Tante Esther pops on a straw
  cloche.
*I know you girls aren't old enough
to vote, but you're welcome to come
  along.*

Rosa shakes
her head, sighs
and I don't feel like
it either, but one thing I do
feel like is getting out
of here so when Rosa heads
down the hall for a bath
I slip on my heels, head
out into the street.

My feet lead
me to the newspaper kiosk
where I study the choices

     from nationalist
              to conservative
     to communist
          to everything in between

wondering what I'm missing
and there it is.

Rather than select
a *Vossische Zeitung*
or any of the regular papers, I opt
for the *Völkischer Beobachter*

official paper
of the Nazi Party

not because I want
to read about them

but because I need to know
what their followers see in them

to try to understand
the enemy and their aim.

THE OTHER SIDE

As soon as I pay
my five Pfennig and start reading
I realize how glad I am Rosa isn't
along to see this.

ADOLF HITLER: MY PROGRAM
AS LONG AS I LIVE, I WILL FIGHT
FOR THE RESURRECTION OF THE GERMAN VOLK,
FOR ITS FUTURE AND ITS GREATNESS.

The problem is that
the future and greatness
of the German Volk is
only for some Germans

  those who think like him

which makes my mind fly
    to Lena
though I quickly dismiss
my doubts about her.

I read on for the details.

  POLITICAL, ECONOMIC, AND CULTURAL
    MARXISM MUST BE ERADICATED!
  SAVING THE FARMING COMMUNITY MEANS
    SAVING THE GERMAN NATION!
  PROTECT WORKING PEOPLE!
  THE STRUGGLE CONTINUES FOR THE NEW REICH,
    FOR FREEDOM AND BREAD!

  Freedom and bread.

My doubts resurface
as a chill passes
through me.

This terrible man knows
what he's doing.
It's not only about Lena.
This is exactly
what people want to hear
and they are going to
                    gobble up
these words
like the bread they need.

I take swift steps
to the nearest trash can, drop
the newspaper inside, wipe
my hands on my skirt, feeling
like they'll never
get clean.

THE PRESENT

Still feeling hopeless, I head
toward Café Lila because
the only good thing
about this day is it's
the day of my weekly secret
songwriting session with Ute.

A block away, I spot

Ute ahead of me, call
out a greeting.

Ute lifts
a hand in a wave, I run
to catch up, we embrace
                    hello

and out of nowhere

three men in blue police uniforms
            emerge
from the shadows
take us in from head to foot
hurl ugly words
our way

                    What have we got here?
                    A man dressed as a woman and
                            a woman as a man?

I curse
my height
exposing me to
unexpected
attack
        curse
their prejudice
declaring Ute

ought not
wear a
suit.

One of the officers runs
a hand over Ute's chest
while another reaches
for my hair, tugs on it
        perhaps expecting a wig to fall
        into his hands.

The pain makes my eyes sting
        not in my roots
        but in my heart
that these policemen
who are supposed to protect
        their citizens
are instead determined
to hurt us.

I don't know how long
the scrutiny goes on

                seconds

                        minutes

        forever

until the third officer steps
in front of them.

Enough, he says.
We're not after individuals
right now
but the clubs themselves.

Excuse me? Ute's mouth
drops open.

The chief's started a campaign
against
amusements
of a homosexual nature.

He sets off
down the block toward
the popular Eldorado club.

Let's go, men.

The others turn to follow him but
the one who pulled my hair now steps
close enough to gather up

a throatful
of spit that he

splatters

over my face before taking
off after the others.

I gasp
too shocked
to say
a word.

Ute extracts
a handkerchief, cleans
me up

        but

nothing
can clean up
        a city
        a country
whose
uniformed officers treat
human beings this way.

My Berlin might
be rough-and-tumble but
this has reached
a new level of ugliness.

        *I never thought
        things would go this far.*

Ute wraps an arm around
my shoulders but
it's no comfort, knowing

things might
only
get
worse.

SPILLING ALL

Ute and I arrive at
the club in silence
both of us casting
cautious glances down
the block before slipping
inside, locking
the door behind us.

Despite everything, we still
need to take advantage of
our time alone to rehearse
the new songs including
the secret one for Rosa
        so close to ready!
but we do so without
our usual pep

and

when the others arrive
     Brigitte
     Rosa
     Lena
they can all tell
something's happened.

We shake
our heads, brush
it off at first

but after a moment
Ute heads for the
bar, takes down
a bottle of whiskey, motions
everyone to join in.

One shot of whiskey down
and Ute's sharing
     those ugly words
     that disconcerting news.

STRENGTH IN NUMBERS

Rosa's visibly shaken
     hands trembling

cheeks pale
and none of us says it
but we all know it

    that to be queer and
    Jewish means
    even more trouble
    in this Germany.

Rosa takes a long
swig of whiskey before
excusing herself and
               disappearing
backstage

right as Emil and Erich arrive
eyebrows raised taking
us all in.

            Who died?

Ute snorts
then, already sounding
almost back to
normal.

          Brigitte speaks
          for us this time.
          Now that Brüning's out

and Papen's lifted the SA ban,
the chief of police is evidently aiming
to keep up with the Brownshirts.

As long as they keep
it out on the streets.

I wouldn't be so sure
about that. Ute shrugs.

I can check with the chief,
Erich says. *He owes me*
a favor or two.

Emil says nothing
but he and Erich join
us in a whiskey, join
us gazing
toward the door
        in apprehension.

CONFESSIONS

We make it through
the night without
incident, all of us
        subdued
and when we finish

cleaning, we pick
up our things, head
out the door.

I walk beside
Rosa, giving her

        the space

she needs, but after a
couple of blocks she slows,
sighs, stops.

            I feel like my world
            is falling apart.

     Not your world.
     I shake my head.
     Our world.

            Same thing.
            Everything I thought
            stable and secure
            is washing away
            like sand at the sea.

I wait, listen.

Tante Esther's situation
the upcoming vote
threats from soldiers
against Jews
against queers.
I feel so alone.

But you aren't alone,
I promise you.

I slip
my hand in hers, show
her I am
here.

JULY 30, 1932
AFTERNOON WALK

A string of anxious
late nights leads
to long mornings and
Rosa's still asleep now
though it's far
past noon but
something pulls
me out of

     the bed
     the flat
     the street

and into action
down Ku'Damm
past people promenading
like nothing's
changed.

I can't help wondering

     which side

       each of them stands on

and I'm so lost
in my thoughts that it takes
me a moment to realize
the girl I just passed
was

     her.

A ROAD MAP

Gretchen's half a block
away by the time I've put

        her face, name, betrayal

together and it takes
me another half a block
     between
    us
for my feelings to crash
into me

       the hurt

         the fear

   the fury

to finally realize
I have nothing left to say
to her
    at all.

MEMORY

Back then
Gretchen was the star

    with the golden future
    ahead of her

and I was nothing but
the supportive girlfriend

    my biggest dream
    the hope

        that hers might someday
        come true

and seeing her again
reminds me of

        the embarrassment
        I was back then

a testament
to how far I've come.

WITHIN REACH

I straighten my dress,
push Gretchen and
everything I can't control
out of my mind
in favor of

the

things
I can

including the potential of
a dazzling future
wrapping Rosa in furs, a
flat of our own, taking
her by the hand on a
whirlwind voyage
by zeppelin.

This diamond-glittery
life courtesy of
the brand-new songs
by Ute and me

cut on the record
Artiphon will surely produce
once we share them.

Before I know it
I've arrived at Café Lila
where I find everyone
already there
expressions equally somber
the lot of them discussing
the *Vossische Zeitung* spread
    over the bar
with the thick, clear headline
about tomorrow's election

  DEFEND YOURSELVES

  WITH THE WEAPON

   OF THE BALLOT!

But there's no time
to add my opinion
because Ute breaks
it up, calls
us to the stage.

Even Rosa's smile for me is
subdued and she says

  nothing

so I squeeze
her hand, hoping
for a chance to
lift her spirits
soon.

PUDDLES

After a long
        melancholy
night in front of
a muted crowd
Rosa and I step
into the alley
out to the street.

It's stopped raining, but
the street shimmers with a
sheen of water as fine as tears.

Rosa leads the
way down the block
our heels echoing
off the buildings.

Streetlamps wink
dimly, painting
patterned shadows

over the street and it's
beautiful and I don't
want to break the magic
but I have to ask Rosa
what's on her mind.

The same as always. She sighs.
Ever since Tante Esther
        lost her job
ever since those police officers
        confronted you in the street
ever since it became clear that
        not only Jewish people like me
        but people like us
                different from the others
        are the enemy of the state.
I don't even know
what we can do
to defend ourselves.

Rosa's words hang
in the air like a
title card in a film.

Heart pounding, I shift
my gaze to meet hers.

The entire city seems

to be under a spell
      asleep for once
and I break the quiet with
       whispered words.

      Maybe instead of defending
      ourselves, we should give in.

                Hilde. Rosa squeezes my hand.
                I'm so lucky to have you.

Her voice chokes
      lips shining
eyes grow hazy
and I forget
everything else.

She takes
a step forward until
we're standing
there in the street just
inches from each other.

                You're an absolute darling.
                She slides her hand
                up my cheek, raises her face.
                My darling.

Time seems to stop
as she leans
toward me.

Our lips touch
gently, she presses
deeper and I do
the same, tasting
her cherry-soft
mouth with
new hunger.

My head swirls
with the taste of

      smoky champagne
      dazzling sparks
      the crispest night

and I can't tell
if the kiss has gone on for
seconds or even minutes when
I take a step
back, try
to catch
my
breath.

Let's go home, shall we?

Let's, I agree, breathless.

Heels pounding, we race
each other the rest of
the way.

Once there, we halt, taking
each other in under
the spectacular canopy of
this night in Berlin
                    unfurled
above us like
black velvet
and
nothing else
in the world
        matters.

CONSTELLATIONS

We rush

up the stairs
        into the flat
                down the hall

where Rosa closes
the door to her room

behind us.

Silent as night, I reach
a hand to Rosa before
we lean in for a kiss as
delicious and luxurious as
the one in the street.

We kiss and kiss
        my legs trembling
until Rosa kicks
off her shoes, undoes
her buttons
        then mine, letting
our dresses
        fall
to the floor.

I tower
in my well-worn
chemise and knickers, wishing
for once I'd spent
some of my earnings on
something pretty.

Rosa steps forward
moonlight
        shining
        over

her fashionable
camiknickers and
once I reach for
the pink silkiness, I forget
all else.

Together, we climb
onto the feather bed, roll
to the center, falling
perfectly into each other
                kissing and touching
until every inch
of my skin tingles and the
room lights up with
thousands of
tiny stars and
we both lie there
        calm
        and
        whisper-still.

JULY 31, 1932
ELECTION DAY

In the morning
secret smiles
giggles
kisses
with Rosa
and I almost can't
believe this is real

       my feelings for her out in the open
               and not only that
      but

             shared

until a much harsher
reality slaps us in the face
at breakfast with
the newspaper headline

    VETO

    THE HOUR OF THE VOTER

challenging readers to use
their ballots to fight
the Nazis

the urgency of the moment casting
thick tension over
    the city
    the household
    my heart.

Adults twenty and older
stream

    in and out

of polling places, while
Rosa and I can't vote
for two more years

can't do anything

    so instead we're
        stuck
           helpless

waiting.

IT'S A DATE

I make
my regular excuse
to Rosa

my need to take
a walk by myself
hurry to Café Lila

where Ute waits for me
            filled
with as much pent-up
energy as I feel

and the pair of us rush
for the piano, run through
all five of our new songs
and this is it
        they're good and
        we know it.

                        Will you set up an appointment
                        with Herr Eisner? Ute asks.

I will. I nod. *But maybe*
we can play Rosa's song here first?

                        Friday night? Ute grins.

Jawohl. I grin back
thrilled to know
something positive awaits
        in the near future.

August 1932

AUGUST 1, 1932
CURIOSITY

Early the next morning, a
commotion erupts
from the street below
before I'm fully awake.

The vote.
Dread fills
me as I scramble
for yesterday's clothes.

Rosa's still sleeping and
Tante Esther isn't up
yet either, the rest of
the building sitting silent.

I press
my lips together, pull
on my things, hurry
out of the flat.

NUMBERS DON'T LIE

Another roar rises
from the street when
I push open the door.

Outside, the air's
cool, all's
peaceful, but when I turn
the corner, a crowd pushes
toward the newsstand.

I speed toward
people holding copies of
the *Berliner Tageblatt,* dig
in my pocket for a coin.

Save your money.
An older gentleman shakes
his newspaper in the air.
Those brutes have gone and won
the most seats!

Brutes?
A young man looks him over
his expression indignant.
Don't listen to him.
It's an incredible victory.
A spectacular day for Germany!

I glance down at the
newspaper he holds:

ON THE LEFT: ON THE RIGHT:

SOCIAL DEMOCRATS: 21.6%   NATIONAL SOCIALISTS: 37.3%

              133 SEATS   230 SEATS

Several other parties are
listed in between
but the Nazis have won
     by far the most
and a quick scan of the article proves
they only had 107 seats the last time.

Now they boast more than
double that.

My insides lurch, weighted
down with doom.

AUGUST 5, 1932
RESPITE

After a few days of
attempting to come to terms
with the election results by
      fretting
      pacing
      worrying
over what will come next
Rosa reminds me
it's Friday, time for
      Shabbat.

Again it's a breath
          exhaled
sharing challah and wine
listening to song and prayer
letting the world fade
away

this moment with
these dear people
      meaning
      everything.

MILITARY EXERCISES

After we get ready
Rosa and I take a detour through
Leipziger Platz before heading
to Café Lila for rehearsal
my mind whirring
until Rosa grips my arm.

I stumble, pull her
into the shadows.

Gas streetlamps light
up the square,
        thrusting
the three or four SA soldiers
into the spotlight.

Pedestrians steer clear
        averting their gazes
as the soldiers wind
up their arms, hurl
                rocks
through the Wertheim department store's
glass display windows, disappear
into the shadows
their laughter echoing
off the walls.

Everyone knows
the owners are Jewish

just like Rosa.

Clutching my hand,
she draws
in a sharp breath like
the weight of
what we've just seen
has landed
on her chest.

TURNING A CORNER

I don't want to wait
to find out what
these brutes will do
next.

Come on.

Keeping to the
shadows, I pull Rosa
away
from the square toward Café Lila.

But something looks different
here, too.

Across the club's façade,
dark paint proclaiming

DEGENERATE CLUB!

The front door's
wide open
            dangling
off its top hinge.

Brigitte and Ute hover
by the door, tools and scrubbing
brushes in hand. I rush
toward them to help.

Lovely surprise
to welcome us tonight.
Ute shrugs.

Rosa remains frozen
beside me, her face
pinched, pale.

I clear
my throat, speak
for both of us.

We saw soldiers vandalizing
Wertheim when we passed
by Leipziger Platz, too.

> *All their favorite scapegoats*
> *in one night,* Ute muses.
> *Busy times for the SA.*

I clutch Rosa's hand
once more
        doubly worried
for her as I'm sure
she is too.

We stare out at the street
through the open door.
The early fall evening has
already closed in,
                shrouding
the street in
dark, sinister shadows.

Brigitte turns
to face us, breaking
the silence as she hands
me a scrubbing brush.

> *Take this and do your best*
> *to get the façade cleaned up.*

Surveying the lot of us,
she wipes her hands on her skirt.
I'm going out to speak to Emil.
This can't go on.

A PLAN

Lena arrives
soon after Brigitte leaves
and we use the time before
we open to get the club back
in shape

    scrubbing graffiti
    making repairs
    reattaching the front door.

Luckily, most of the interior
is still clear and usable
and everything else looks
normal when Brigitte returns
with Emil and Erich.

Erich found us a new place.
Emil pulls us together
in a close circle.
After tonight, we're moving
to the basement of a bar

in the heart
of Nollendorfplatz.

It's only two blocks from here,
Erich adds.
I'm signing the lease tomorrow.

I glance at the empty stage.
This is it, then?

Assuming all goes well,
we'll be open for business
next week, Emil says.
Erich and Kurt and I
will carry everything over
in the morning
and get it prettied up.

Wunderbar!
Ute slaps Emil on the back.
Sounds like a perfect plan.

We'll let the patrons know
tonight, Brigitte says.
I'll write up notes
with the new address,
you girls will slip them
to the regulars.

Only hand out the notes
to people you know, Emil says.
Trust no one else.

I shiver.
How much has changed
in a week.

Ute nods. *Let's work together*
and make it count.

Indeed, Brigitte says.
What do we have
if not each other?

I squeeze
Rosa's hand.
The circle breaks
up, and everyone
                scatters
like billiard balls.

Everyone except Lena.

I turn for a look over
my shoulder. Rooted
to the floor, Lena stares
at the velvet curtain out front

flapping

in the warm August
breeze as though all the
answers in the world are
there, just beyond reach.

MOST DAZZLING GIRL

It doesn't take
long to find
      Katja and Käthe
      Herr Neumann
      the Vogel sisters
      other close girlfriends
slip notes into their hands.
Soon enough
it's showtime.

                Ready? Rosa stubs out
                her cigarette.

I peer through the
spotlight over the smoky
tables as Ute heads
for the piano

and I finally remember

tonight's the night
for Rosa's song

and I can't think of a better
antidote to this gloom
around us.

With a nod to Ute, who begins
the lovely melody, I step
toward the microphone, sing
the first words.

> *I slipped in here that first night*
> *just looking for escape*
> *but I stepped into a dream.*
> *You burst into a sweet smile*
> *so full of joy and life*
> *but things aren't all that they seem.*

My voice cracks
but a sidewise glance at
Rosa energizes me.

> *In this magical place,*
> *with this magical girl,*
> *all that I ever wished for sings*
> *right in this very room*
> *right in my very heart*
> *wrapped in your butterfly wings.*

One more glance at Rosa
      her eyes sparkling.

      For you are the most marvelous girl
      one who makes me whirl.
      Your heart is what I hope to win,
      most dazzling girl in Berlin.

      For I've fallen so hard and so fast
      feelings true and vast.
      I'll prove my love, please let me in,
      most dazzling girl in Berlin.

A roar of applause bursts
from the very back of
the audience near the front
doors of the club, sending
a thrill through me

      but

a moment later
I realize
it's not
applause
at all.

A SWARM

Angry-faced
soldiers push
their way through
the tables, all
nightsticks and
biceps and
elbows.

I cry out, and
my voice screeches
through the microphone
        reverberates
across the room.

Ute hops up, knocking
over the piano bench.

The men shove
patrons aside, overturn
tables, smash
bottles and
glasses to the ground.
All around the
room, people scream.

                    Run! Brigitte shouts.

The customers near
the door push
past the soldiers out
to the street, but
we stand frozen
in the spotlight as
more men spill
in from the back
entrance, cornering us.

Emil comes barreling
out from behind
the bar and
I watch, helpless, as
one of the soldiers strikes
Emil on the head with a club
then Erich, who tumbles
onto his knees
at his side.

Once first blood's drawn,
the rest of them attack,
toothy as sharks.

Rosa launches
        herself off
        the stage onto
        the back of
        the closest soldier.

Brigitte whacks
     anyone who dares
     approach the bar with
     a broom handle.

I grab
the microphone
like a spear, sending
another painful
squawk through
the loudspeakers as
more soldiers proceed
through the front door
led by a man who parts
the chaos in front of
him with his
appearance.

Lena's father.

                We are shutting down
                this illegal, immoral club,
                his voice booms.

He steps forward into
the spotlight, another
soldier close at his heels.

Tall as a poplar, with

a swath of blond hair falling
in his face.

BOMBSHELL

It's Kurt.

Against the bar, Emil
and Erich stare
at him, mouths dropping
open in identical Os
of disbelief

      but

Lena marches
across the room toward
Kurt, planting
herself at his side

      another punch
      in the gut

           one that hurts
           even more.

Their expressions remain
blank, like they were

never
part of us at all.

I feel sick.
How could she?

Lena's father marches
forward, lips curling
in a sneer.

Our city has had quite enough
of degenerate places like this.
This is not our new Berlin.
Let's go, men!

His men
                including Kurt
thrust toward us while

        shouts
                        screams
            cries

ring out across the room.

All the while Lena holds
her position at the door, arms
crossed, doing

                    nothing
to stop it

          nothing
          to help us
at all.

FINALE

One of the soldiers swings
his club in a wild
circle at Rosa, knocking
her to the ground.

I jump off the stage.

          Nein!

                              Enough! Lena's father bellows.
                              The soldiers snap to attention.
                              This club is closed.
                              He sweeps out to the street
                                        followed
                              by the rest of his mob
                              including Lena.

Rosa lies
unmoving.

I push forward,
can't get through
the debris between us
even after the
soldiers retreat.

Finally I make
it around the edge of the
room to her, to find
Rosa's dark bob slick
with wetness from a cut
at her temple, her nose
crooked at an odd angle.

Nein, nein, nein.
My throat constricts.

This
cannot
be
happening.

BRUTES

The shrill note of
a scream pierces
my ears like a
shard of glass and

it's my scream and
I hear it but
I don't feel it
in my throat or
in my lungs and
I don't care and
simply can't stop.

The scream continues until
my ears ring with the terrible
sound of my voice,
something, anything
has to end the horror of
this night.

Rosa lies
before me, limp and
shattered.

My head pounds
as I struggle to
swallow
breathe
think.

Rosa!

I lean over her
wilted flower form

squeezing her hands, kissing
her forehead, but
she's rag-doll unresponsive.

Panic grips
me by the
shoulders, shaking
me to my core, spilling
out my eyes and over
my cheeks.

IN SHOCK

Sirens sound
from the street, but
I barely register
what's happening when
orderlies and police officers enter.

The police inspect
the scene, the orderlies carry off
                    Brigitte
            the Vogel sisters
        others who were injured.

        Over here!
        I raise a hand.

But movement and voices carry
on around me as though
        nothing
happened, as though Rosa
        this beautiful, jolly girl
isn't in mortal danger.

I steal another glance at
        Rosa's nose
        blood flowing down
        one side of her face
        cheeks pale as paper.

Her face looks ghastly, yet
over the choking
odor of blood,
a faint scent of
gardenia rises
to my nose.

                    Excuse me. One of the orderlies
                    stands right in front of me.

        Bitte. I tug on his arm.
        You have to help her.

He checks her breathing
puts pressure on the cut
touches her nose.

His expression serious, he nods
to his companion, they slide
Rosa onto a stretcher.

Ute appears
at my side, wraps
an arm around
me, gently tugging
me away.

My throat swells
under the weight
of a friendly arm, but even if
it's meant to be calming
it's stifling, not calm
and I struggle
to free myself and
to breathe and
hold myself upright.

TURNING THE TABLES

A policeman waves
Ute over.

> *You there.*
> *Were you here*
> *during the bar brawl?*

Bar brawl? Ute frowns.
A group of soldiers
pushed their way in
like they owned this place.

We were alerted about
depraved nightlife going on here.
The owners are responsible.

My head snaps up.
Haven't we been through
        enough
without this, too?

Excuse me? Ute blinks.

                Amusements of a homosexual
                        nature
                are now subject to
                stricter controls.
                We're taking these two
                down to the station now.
                The officer gestures
                to Emil and Erich
                being led out of the club
                        both of them pressing
                        bar towels over
                        their injuries.

I don't think you understand.
A group of soldiers came in
and destroyed the place.

       That's not our concern.
       The policeman closes
       his notebook.
       Now if you'll excuse me.
       He nods, leaves.

Beside me, the orderlies lift
the stretcher.

       They'll notify her next of kin
       with any news.

    Wait!

I bolt
toward the stretcher.
Emil and Erich have
already been escorted
to a waiting car out front but
I can't let Rosa be taken
away from me like this.

I lean
over the stretcher, take
her into my arms, kiss

her cheek, my tears mingling
with the metallic
taste on her skin.

Ute scribbles
Tante Esther's telephone
number on a scrap of
paper, hands it to them.

The orderlies nod
and without another glance,
the two of them sweep
the stretcher away.

I fear
my future will
only taste
of blood and salt.

SLEEPWALKER

I move
as though in
a dream
      a nightmare.

I'd like to support

Ute
        who looks as lost

                as I feel
but

the two of us are
clearly so

                        overwhelmed

simply surveying
the aftermath
of this night.

THE MESSENGER

I bid
farewell, head
for Rosa's home
in a daze.

My footsteps slow
as I climb
the stairs to
the flat, each step a
blow to my heart as my

mind considers the words
to say to Tante Esther
inside.

But there's no use putting
it off, especially if
I want to catch
her before she retires
so I slip
my key in the lock.

You're home early!

Tante Esther's surprise
quickly turns to
        dismay
when she catches
a glimpse of
my face.

What is it?

I tell her
        quick
like a
cut to the bone

and I can tell
it hurts her

as much as it
hurts me

and

there's nothing more
to say

we just sit
there on the
settee the rest of
the night waiting
for the
telephone to
ring.

AUGUST 6, 1932
CRASH

I must've finally fallen
asleep because the
sound of the telephone
    ringing
jolts me awake where
I'm sitting, my
head twisted
at an uncomfortable
angle.

Tante Esther's already
crossing the room to
pick up and by
the time I'm sitting
properly, her
voice cracks
out a greeting.

Static, a voice
from the other end.

                      Gott sei Dank.

Tante Esther thanks God and
so do I and I'm wide

awake now and waiting
for whatever details
they share.

But Tante Esther doesn't
say much more than
     ja
     ja
     ja
to whatever they're telling
her from the other end of
the line and I must
     wait, wait, wait
until she hangs
up, turns to face
me.

                         She's fine.
                         She's going to be
                           fine.
                         They're observing her
                         this morning
                         since it's a head injury
                         but we can go get her
                         in the afternoon.
                         She's fine.
                         She's going to be
                           fine.

And with these
words we explode
into tears, sobs, howls
making our way toward
each other for the
hug we both wish
we were giving Rosa

     right
     now.

DOING SOMETHING

Tante Esther goes
off to her bedroom to try
to sleep, but I can't sit
around
       waiting
until the afternoon

I have to do
something.

I turn
to the only distraction that
can possibly help, head
to Herr Eisner's studio
to request an appointment

for the recording session
             with Ute.

After the trip
      across the city
      into the familiar building
I approach the door,
my footfalls echoing
off the walls.

Dark.

The recording studio's dark,
the name scratched clean
off the glass door.
It can't be.

I hurry closer, try
the handle. Locked.
I pound
on the glass pane with
my knuckles.
No response.

A door down the hall clicks
open, and I bend
over my pocketbook, try
to compose myself.

Looking for
Artiphon-Record?

A young man in a suit pokes
his head out the door.

I frown, nod.

They've moved on.
The man puffs up
his cheeks in sympathy.

I gasp, my hand pops
up to my mouth.

Moved on?

The management decided not to rent
to Herr Eisner's kind anymore, and —

What? I cut him off.
What do you mean, his kind?

I step
        forward
into the light.

The man's gaze sweeps
the corridor.

You know. He lowers
his voice. *Jewish.*

Jewish.
Like Rosa
like Tante Esther.

If you'd like, though, he left me
his contact information. Perhaps
it would be of some use to you?

I nod, step
toward his door, hover
there as he shuffles
through his desk, writes
something on a scrap of paper.

There you are.
He'd been thinking
of leaving anyway,
but the rental being canceled
on him was the last straw.
He pauses.
He was quite a nice fellow.
For a Jew, I mean.

I stiffen.

I'm sure he still is.

I glance at the address
Champs-Élysées 50, Paris.

Not even in Germany,
much less Berlin.

I slip
the paper into my handbag.

I appreciate your help
in tracking him down.

With a nod, I spin
on my heel, picking
up speed down the hallway
until I exit to the street.
Once there, I look at
the address once more.

Paris.

I've only ever
lived in Berlin but
there's a whole wide world
out there.

I slip the paper
back into my pocket
for someday.

FAMILY

After the
disappointment
at the studio on top
of last night's trauma
I take a chance and stop
by Café Lila to see
if anyone's there.

The door's shut
it appears
        dark
from the street but when
I jiggle
the handle, the door gives
way so I step inside
to find two huddled
figures whispering
behind the bar.

I squint, trying
to decide whether
I should enter.

                        Hilde?

I let out a breath.

Ute?

And we're

         speeding
across the floor toward
each other, spilling
our news, sharing our
relief that at least
all of us are
still alive.

PLANS

The other figure steps
out of the shadows then

    and

it's Brigitte
a determined set to her jaw.

I have to
apologize.

      This is all my fault.
      I never should've vouched for Lena.

         How were you to know?

Brigitte asks. *Besides,*
it was Kurt's doing as much as hers.
She shakes her head.
Emil treated that boy like a son.

> *Listen, Hilde,*
> *don't beat yourself up*
> *about it,* Ute says.
> *It's a good thing*
> *to believe the best in people,*
> *I hope you still will.*

I'm not sure I will
      not anymore
but I certainly want the best
for my Café Lila family.

> *What about you two?*
> *What are you planning?*

> *We're going to get*
> *Emil and Erich*
> *out of jail,* Ute says.

Her words make it sound
as easy as pouring
a drink, but then
Brigitte spills
the details.

It'll mean paying a bribe
but I've just arranged
to meet with one of
Erich's associates
to do that.

If anyone can get this done,
it's most decidedly
the two of you.

Church bells down the
block chime
the hour.

Ach so! Tante Esther and I
need to go get
Rosa from the hospital.

Good luck, Ute says.

You too.
I pause.
I'll be thinking
of you all.

TRUE BEAUTY

Tante Esther and I stand
in the corridor just
outside Rosa's hospital room
peek in the window.

The corners of Rosa's lips
        sink
        downward
                pulling
attention from her injuries

nose
        still swollen
cut at her hairline
        stitched up
her eyes
        dull and sad.

I already know
it'll be difficult to convince
such a charming girl
that it was much more than
        her looks
that made her so lovely
all along.

Something squeezes
inside my chest.
    Rosa's smiles
      her cheery outlook
      her kisses.

How lucky
we once were.

But perhaps a
small bit of that
luck remains
for us.

I press
my lips together, step
inside.

A LONG ROAD

Rosa clears
her throat from
where she sits
dressed and waiting
on a hospital bed.

I'm ready to go now.

I put on my
brightest smile.

You're as dazzling as ever.

Of course she is!
Tante Esther says.

I don't agree
at all.

A tired smile passes
over Rosa's lips but
doesn't reach
her eyes.

We'll get you home,
Tante Esther says.
We'll get you safe.

But Rosa shakes
her head.

I don't know
if I'll ever feel safe
in Berlin again.

And all of a
sudden I know
just
what
she
needs
and I make up my mind
to tell her
as soon as
the time is right.

BROKEN

Back home, Rosa rests
for minutes, hours, days
making me wonder
if she'll ever feel
whole again

but I'm itching to show
her a way back
to herself, so on her third
day home I open
Rosa's wardrobe, thumb
through
      silky dresses
      hats
      a fur coat

and turn to her, prepared
to share
          my idea.

Happy-go-lucky Rosa
lurks in that wardrobe, frozen
in time

but

the real Rosa flops
on the bed, a faint
scent of gardenia floating
loosely in the air.

Her hips and
shoulders form
      soft hills
making me feel
like I must tiptoe
up to her.

    Rosa.

I whisper
the word so softly
I barely hear
it myself
but Rosa does.

Her eyelids flutter
open as she lets
out a languid sigh.

*Nothing will ever
be the same again.*

Her words are
the perfect
        segue
to the thoughts I want
to share.

    Liebchen.

I slip an arm around
Rosa's back, slide
the other up her neck.
My fingers brush
her chin.

    *You're exactly right
        which is why
    we need to leave Berlin
            as soon as
    possible.*

        Leave Berlin?

She meets my gaze
            her injured nose still
            angry and swollen
not agreeing to come
but not saying no
either.

I wrap
my arms around
her once more.

            All I wanted before
            was some sense of
                            home
            a feeling of
                    heart and
                    happiness.

I pause, remembering
            my old neighborhood
            the orphanage
            Café Lila.

            But I realized it's not
            about the place at all.
            My home
            is with

                    you

wherever you are
and I hope that's enough
for you too.

JAWOHL

Rosa's response is a
     kiss
     hug
     wild grin

and the two of us are
          going places.

AUGUST 12, 1932
PACKING

I place
my recording disc
on top of

                 dresses
                         underthings
cosmetics

snap the case shut.

The wad of money I've saved
       bit by bit
over months at the club goes
deep into my pocketbook
next to
       my papers
            hopes
            dreams.

Rosa fills a larger case with
clothing, photographs, a jewelry box
softly touching
each item she leaves
           behind.

Our bags packed
we head down the hall for
one last meal with
Tante Esther.

BREAKFAST

Tante Esther already sits
at the table with
a basket of Brötchen
before her

and Rosa rushes
for her, crushing
her in a tight hug.

*Are you sure you won't
come along?*

Tante Esther shakes her head.
*I have another job interview this week.
High hopes for this one!*

We wish her all the best
of course
even as she turns
her attention
to us.

WELL-WISHING

Tante Esther breaks into
our wishes for her, shakes
a finger, makes a request.

> *The two of you are in love*
> *and off on a grand adventure.*
> *I don't want tears but joy.*

> Rosa sniffles, says,
> *As long as you promise*
> *to come to us*
> *if things get worse here.*

Tante Esther
nods
      promises

and we three reach
for one another
glad to have had this time

      as family.

FAREWELL

Once breakfast is over
I can barely contain
my excitement.
In only a few hours
Rosa and I will be
making our way to
parts unknown
            together.

She and I each slip a
pile of money across
the table toward
Tante Esther.

To tide you over for now,
Rosa says.
*But I hope you'll join us
wherever we end up.*

Berlin is my home, she says.
*I simply can't imagine
leaving it.
But we'll see.*

Another last check of
the flat and we're ready.

Everyone comes by to bid
us farewell

Brigitte and Ute
Emil and Erich
sprung free by the combination
of fat bribes and
promises to keep
to the shadows

all of them lined
up like fans waiting
for autographs.

I stand beside Rosa at
the entrance to the
sitting room surveying
faces full of hope.

These dear, dear people.
How I wish
they were coming
with us.

*You'd better drop us a line
once you're there,* Ute says,
giving us each a sloppy kiss.
Wherever there is.

*Perhaps we'll join you
one day,* Brigitte adds.
Or at least come visit.

Emil nods, cheeks puffed
up, a worry line etched
across his forehead.

*Keep your eyes peeled
for a good spot
for Café Lila,* Erich says.
*Now that our new location
isn't safe either
we're mulling over our options.*

Emil finally breaks, letting
a stream of tears slip
down his face.

*Don't forget
you'll always
have a home
with us.*

Erich wraps an arm
around his shoulders,
Tante Esther dabs her eyes
with a handkerchief.

I'll miss you so much.
She pats Rosa's hand.

                         Me too. Rosa squeezes her
                         in a tight embrace.

The stale air in the flat
suddenly suffocates
me, and I have to go.

        Ready?

I turn
to Rosa.

                         Wiedersehen, Rosa says.

I echo
her good-bye a
moment later and

we're
gone.

THE WHISTLE

Halfway down the stairs, I turn
back for one last look at

the door to the flat and
the magic I found there

    getting to know
         this girl
  falling in love
  finding a home

     hopes
         dreams
future

combined in one precious
bubble floating
skyward.

Rosa and I walk toward the
Bahnhof Zoologischer Garten
in silence until she pulls
a coin from her pocket.

       Where are we going?
       Should we flip for it?

   Nowhere could be worse than here.

       You're right, she agrees.
       Wait. She stops herself.

It's true now, but
ugly as Berlin has become,
it'll always hold
a firm corner of my heart.
It's where my family's from.
It's where we met.
And where you sang me
the loveliest song.

She squeezes
my hand and I flush
warm to my toes.

The station bustles with
        harried businessmen in hats
                rushing for their trains
        women in lipstick waiting
                for a special someone.

A few Brownshirts loiter
talking among themselves
        gazes fixed
on the passing crowd.
I wouldn't mind if I never saw
any of them again.

I lift my gaze to the big
board of departures.

Our choices in the next hour
    Köln
    Paris
    Frankfurt.

Paris, where the man from
Artiphon-Record went.

    Perhaps we don't really need
    to flip.

The Köln train closes
its doors, whistles
its horn, and a series of
clicks and clacks shuffle
the letters on the board, moving
the next city to the top
of the list.
I point.

    Paris?

        Jawohl. That is, mais oui.
        Rosa grins once again
        with the dazzling smile
        that first captured my heart.

GOOD-BYE, BERLIN

With a quick nod,
I leave
my case with Rosa, march
to the counter, purchase
two one-way tickets.

The man hands
me the tickets.

Gleis zwei.

He points
toward track two.

I lead Rosa past
the giant locomotive to
the second-class passenger
cars, finding
our assigned seats in
the already crowded space.

Evidently we aren't
the only ones who want
to escape Berlin.

Ten minutes later, the
train whistles

its horn, pulls
out of the station.

We've made it.
We're really leaving.

Perhaps one day
we'll return, but
for now, I lean
my head against
the window, taking
in my surroundings
as the train slowly picks
up speed, lumbering
through the city, passing
      tenements
        row houses
        churches
        seedy bars.

White light reflects
off the cloudy sky, casting
the shadows of the
buildings in a silvery glow.

There's only one Berlin
      the only city
           I've ever known

but it now lies
in my past.

Not long before, I felt
like the luckiest
girl in the world, basking
in the arms of a jolly girl.

Now we've both
changed, but somehow
I feel even luckier
than before.

Perhaps Berlin will
change again someday.
Perhaps it'll become
the glorious place
the cozy home
it once was.

But for now, all I have left
of Berlin is this
moment, when it peeks
its grimy face out from
under the clouds

and says
        good-bye.

AUTHOR'S NOTE

INSPIRATION

The city of Berlin — especially the Berlin of the Weimar Republic era — has fascinated me for a very long time. There is simply so much to love about it: the music, the films, the fashions. But there was much more beyond the glitz.

The Weimar Republic spanned the years between World War I and World War II (1918–1933), a time of economic instability and hyperinflation that led to unemployment, poverty, and hunger. Politically, it signaled the end of the monarchy and the onset of a precarious democracy that was nearing its end in 1932, when *The Most Dazzling Girl in Berlin* takes place. But before the Nazi Party took full power in 1933, Berliners enjoyed freedoms unlike any they'd experienced before.

In particular, this was a glorious and liberating time for all manner of queer people, who had their pick of venues where they could celebrate among friends and outsiders alike. Travel guides to Berlin at the time highlighted clubs in different parts of the city that catered to various groups where residents and tourists could find their homes away from home among like-minded people.

But if you're familiar with the 1972 film *Cabaret*, based on Christopher Isherwood's *Berlin Stories*, you know that "life is a cabaret" until it's not.

While in hindsight we know a terrible crackdown was coming for Berliners in 1933, my aim here was to show those last months of *before*, when trouble was obviously brewing but when people were still able to cautiously enjoy their freedom, live in the moment, and hold hope for their future. To me, this time has felt very relevant, even parallel in some ways, to life today in the United States, where certain parts of the country still impose restrictions on individuals based on gender and/or sexual orientation and where it's still dangerous to be out and free; but at the same time many communities and institutions such as schools and libraries support queer kids and teens, sometimes when home might not be a safe space.

This kind of openness — of welcome — is incredibly important for queer teens. Queer individuals might be at any point on their journey throughout their lives, and the freedom and time needed to explore one's identity should be not only allowed but encouraged. In this story, Hilde has no doubts about her sexuality, but she still needs to find her people, and the sort of family she falls in with at Café Lila is what I wish for every queer teen today, no matter when they decide they belong.

FACT OR FICTION

My main characters, including Hilde, Rosa, and even Café Lila herself, are all fictional. But the historical backdrop, political events, and specific cultural references are factual, and I did my very best to include as many details as I could about queer clubs in Schöneberg at the time to bring the Café Lila family to life. Curt Moreck's *Ein Führer durch das lasterhafte Berlin: Das deutsche Babylon 1931*, Franz Hessel's *Walking in Berlin: A Flaneur in the Capital*, and several of the essays in Michael Bollé's *Eldorado: Homosexuelle Frauen und Männer in Berlin 1850–1950* provided excellent glimpses into the hundreds of queer venues in the city at the time, while memoirs such as Charlotte Wolff's and Claire Waldoff's and essays such as those in Claudia Schoppmann's *Days of Masquerade: Life Stories of Lesbians During the Third Reich* included personal experiences from lesbians living in the city in the era.

My references to celebrities, films, songs, and books from the time include actresses Marlene Dietrich and Louise Brooks, singer Claire Waldoff, the 1931 film *Mädchen in Uniform*, the 1919 novel *Der Skorpion*, and, last but not least, the 1920 song "Das Lila Lied." Each one of these played an important role in the LGBTQ community in Weimar-era Berlin, and each definitely deserves a closer look today for anyone interested in learning more.

Most of the newspaper headlines I included were from the *Vossische Zeitung*, a liberal Berlin newspaper that published journalists such as Kurt Tucholsky (an author whose books were among the first to be burned by the Nazis in 1933), and a couple of great sources I relied on for visuals from the time were Torsten Palmér and Hendrik Neubauer's *The Weimar Republic Through the Lens of the Press* and Christian Ferber's *Berliner illustrirte Zeitung: Zeitbild, Chronik, Moritat für Jedermann 1892–1945*. There are also plenty of films from the era that clearly show what it was like to live in Berlin at the time (see below for several favorites). For a modern but excellent take on Weimar-era Berlin, be sure to check out *Babylon Berlin*, a German TV series available on Netflix.

A few specific liberties I took in depicting the era: the song "Regentropfen, die an dein Fenster klopfen" by Emil Palm and Josef Hochleitner wasn't actually first recorded until 1935; the youth rally Hilde stumbles on at Leipziger Platz is modeled after one that took place in Potsdam in October 1932; Hermann Eisner was the founder of Artiphon-Record, and though he died in 1927, his company continued until the Nazis shut it down in 1932. He's buried in the Weißensee Jewish cemetery in Berlin.

LEGACY

Today we have the hindsight to know what was coming for queer people and their clubs in Berlin. The action taken was swift once the Nazis came to power in 1933. Queer organizations were disbanded, presses were ordered to cease publication, and several of the most prominent clubs were shut down. Some of the smaller venues continued to operate into 1934 or even 1935, but by then, many people had gone underground or left Berlin entirely. At first, like Hilde and Rosa, many escaping Nazi persecution made Paris their destination, though Jewish people would soon be in danger there as well when Germany invaded in 1940.

Today Berlin is once again a thriving metropolis with celebrations of queer life evident both in Schöneberg and in other parts of town, but signs of its former glory are hard to find. The popular Eldorado club on Motzstraße is now a supermarket, a plaque commemorates the apartment building where Christopher Isherwood lived, and a single column remains on Bülowstraße as a reminder of the Nationalhof, a glamorous ballroom where queer dances were held.

Luckily, we have the memories of queer individuals who experienced the Weimar Republic in Berlin, along with films, photos, and other archives to remind us of this heyday. These snapshots, along with our own imaginations, can conjure up ghosts from bygone days taking strolls over cobblestone sidewalks and dancing the night away behind velvet curtains.

ACKNOWLEDGMENTS

I'm still amazed that I'll soon get to hold this, my second published novel, in my hands. Just like with my debut, *White Rose,* I had a lot of support over a lot of years with this particular book, and once again, I hope beyond hope that I don't forget anyone here, because I couldn't have done it without all of you.

First off, a huge thank-you once again to Kwame Alexander and Margaret Raymo for helping me turn this book into everything I'd hoped it would become. Being part of Versify is like being part of a family, and you all are the best family. Thank you also to the entire Clarion and Versify team for all the support, including Elizabeth Agyemang and Ciera Burch; Ana Novaes and Kaitlin Yang for the beautiful cover; Mary Magrisso, Erika West, and Margaret Wimberger for the eagle eyes; and to John Sellers, Sammy Brown, and Emma Gordon and everyone else in sales, marketing, and publicity for all that you do. A huge thank-you as well to my agent, Roseanne Wells, for helping me shape this story into the queer love letter it is, no matter how many times it took to get it right (dear reader, it was a lot of times). Thank you also to my sensitivity readers, for whose detailed feedback I am eternally grateful.

Likewise, a huge thank-you to my critique partners and readers who have all helped me make this story better. To Monica Ropal, I can say here what I didn't want to spoil in the dedication: this one is for you not only because of the number of times you read it, but because, thanks to you, this book has probably the happiest ending I am capable of writing. And to Marley Teter, who read this story a ridiculous number of times as well, thank you so very much for all your thoughts and support and love along the way. The same goes to Shari Green and Beth Smith — so many thanks, and I love you both so very much. To others who've given oh-so-helpful feedback: Michelle Mason, Kerri Maher, Rachael Romero, Rebecca Caprara, Catherine Egan, Carla Cullen, Marieke Nijkamp, Jen Malone, JRo Brown, and the LitWits — Joan and Julie and Natalie — thank you, thank you, thank you. To Sarah Guillory for your fantastic mentorship in the 2014 Pitch Wars and to the amazing 2014 Pitch Wars class. To the Highlights 2017 verse novel faculty — Kathy Erskine, Alma Fullerton, and Padma Venkatraman — as well as my fellow participants. To my fellow early risers at #5amWritersClub and history nerds at #HFChitChat. And to the amazing opportunity at Hedgebrook and to my beloved Hedgewitches — Sherri L. Smith, Stacey Lee, Nidhi Chanani, Laura Ruby, Brandy Colbert, and Christine Day — I still treasure every moment of our days together in those magical woods!

On the research side, thank you to the staff at the Spinnboden Lesbenarchiv und Bibliothek and to the Frauentour experts in Berlin who answered my questions, and to Claudia Schoppmann for the special help and extensive list of sources to study. Thank you also to all the YA authors today who've written queer stories about the past, and to Dahlia Adler at LGBTQ Reads for "queering up my bookshelves." A special thanks to Nita Tyndall for sharing this Berlin research journey!

To the non-writerly people in my life: to Rosanne Samson for keeping me grounded (and, as always, for the snacks), to Gerhard Feichtinger for the musical brainstorming and composing, and to Matt and Catherine for all the support. Most special thanks to

Megan for the photo expedition to Schöneberg before I could get over there, and to Dad, Bernardo, Lyra, and Violeta for letting me fill our entire Berlin itinerary with history (but also for pulling me out of my research and into the present day from time to time).

Finally, thanks to *you*, reader, for picking up this book and stepping back into a past Berlin where all kinds of love were possible.

SELECTED SOURCES

SOURCES IN ENGLISH

Beachy, Robert. *Gay Berlin*. New York: Alfred A. Knopf, 2014.

Hessel, Franz. *Walking in Berlin: A Flaneur in the Capital*. Translated by Amanda DeMarco. London: Scribe Publications, 2016.

Isherwood, Christopher. *The Berlin Stories*. New York: New Directions Books, 1963.

Jelavich, Peter. *Berlin Cabaret*. Cambridge, MA: Harvard University Press, 1993.

Lybeck, Marti. Desiring Emancipation: New Women and Homosexuality in Germany, 1890–1933. Albany: State University of New York Press, 2014.

Palmér, Torsten, and Hendrik Neubauer. *The Weimar Republic Through the Lens of the Press*. Translated by Peter Barton, Mark Cole, and Susan Cox. Cologne: Könemann Verlagsgesellschaft mbH, 2000.

Schoppmann, Claudia. Days of Masquerade: Life Stories of Lesbians During the Third Reich. New York: Columbia University Press, 1996.

Tamagne, Florence. *A History of Homosexuality in Europe*. Volumes 1 and 2: *Berlin, London, Paris, 1919–1939*. New York: Algora Publishing, 2006.

Tucholsky, Kurt. *Berlin! Berlin! Dispatches from the Weimar Republic*. Translated by Cindy Opitz. New York: Berlinica Publishing, 2013.

Wolff, Charlotte. *Hindsight: An Autobiography*. London: Quartet Books, 1980.

SOURCES IN GERMAN

Berliner Tageblatt (Berlin), February–August 1932.

Bollé, Michael (Berlin Museum). *Eldorado: Homosexuelle Frauen und Männer in Berlin 1850–1950, Geschichte, Alltag und Kultur* [Eldorado: Homosexual women and men in Berlin 1850–1950]. Berlin: Frölich & Kaufmann, 1984.

Ferber, Christian. *Berliner illustrierte Zeitung: Zeitbild, Chronik, Moritat für Jedermann, 1892-1945* [Berlin Illustrated Newspaper: Picture of the times, chronicle, street ballad for everyone, 1892-1945]. Berlin: Ullstein Verlag, 1985.

Moreck, Curt. *Ein Führer durch das lasterhafte Berlin: Das deutsche Babylon 1931* [A guide through depraved Berlin: The German Babylon 1931]. 2nd ed. Berlin-Brandenburg: Be.bra verlag GmbH, 2018.

Schwules Museum. www.schwulesmuseum.de.

Spinnboden Lesbenarchiv und Bibliothek Berlin. www.spinnboden.de.

Völkischer Beobachter (Berlin), February–August 1932.

Vossische Zeitung (Berlin), February–August 1932.

Waldoff, Claire. *Weeste noch . . . ! Aus meinen Erinnerungen* [Do you still know . . . ! From my memoirs]. Düsseldorf: Progress-Verlag, 1953.

Weirauch, Anna Elisabet. *Der Skorpion* [The scorpion]. Berlin: Askanischer Verlag, 1919.

FILMS

Dudow, Slatan, dir. *Kuhle wampe oder: Wem gehört die Welt?* [Kuhle Wampe, or Who owns the world?]. Berlin: Prometheus Film, 1932.

Fosse, Bob, dir. *Cabaret*. Hollywood: Allied Artists, 1972.

Lang, Fritz, dir. *M: Eine Stadt sucht einen Mörder* [M: A city searches for a murderer]. Berlin: Nero-Film AG, 1931.

May, Joe, dir. *Asphalt* [Asphalt]. Babelsberg: UFA, 1929.

Pabst, G. W., dir. *Die Büchse der Pandora* [Pandora's box]. Berlin: Nero-Film AG, 1929.

Ruttmann, Walther, dir. *Berlin: Die Sinfonie einer Großstadt* [Berlin: Symphony of a metropolis]. Berlin: Deutsche Vereins-Film, 1928.

Sagan, Leontine, dir. *Mädchen in Uniform* [Girls in uniform]. Berlin: Deutsche Film-Gemeinschaft, 1931.

Siodmak, Robert, and Edgar Ulmer. *Menschen am Sonntag* [People on Sunday]. Berlin: Filmstudio Berlin, 1930.

Tykver, Tom, Achim von Borries, and Henk Handloegten. *Babylon Berlin*. Berlin: X-Filme Creative Pool, 2017.

von Sternberg, Josef. *Der blaue Engel* [The blue angel]. Berlin: UFA, 1930.

GLOSSARY

Alle meine Entchen schwimmen auf dem See: All my ducklings swim on the lake

Auf Wiedersehen: Good-bye

Bahnhof: Train station

Beobachter: Observer

Berlinerisch: Berlin dialect

Bitte: Please

Brötchen: Rolls

Buchladen: Bookstore

Danke: Thanks

Das Lila Lied: The Lavender Song

Deutscher: German or Germans

Ein Kuß, ein Kuß: A kiss, a kiss

Es gibt nur ein Berlin!: There's only one Berlin!

Gedächtnis-Kirche: Memorial church

Gemüseladen: Greengrocer

Geschlossen: Closed

Gleis: Track

Gott sei Dank: Thank God

Guten Abend: Good evening

Guten Morgen: Good morning

Hakenkreuz: Swastika

Hausfrauen: Housewives

Herein!: Come in!

Herr: Mr.

Ich bin von Kopf bis Fuß auf Liebe eingestellt: I'm from head to foot set on love

Ja: Yes

Jawohl: Absolutely

Kaiser: Emperor

Kaufhaus des Westens: Department Store of the West

Kinderleicht: Easy as pie

Liebchen: Sweetheart

Liebe Hilde: Dear Hilde

Mädchen in Uniform: Girls in uniform

Mutti: Mom

Nein: No

Pfennig: Penny or cents

Platz: Place or plaza

Raus!: Out!

Raus mit den Männern: Out with the men

Regentropfen, die an mein Fenster klopfen: Raindrops that patter on my window

Reichsmark: Weimar Republic currency

Schwester: Sister

Skorpion: Scorpion

Straße: Street

Sturmabteilung: Storm troopers

Tageblatt: Journal

Tante: Aunt

U-Bahn: Subway

Verlag: Publisher

Volk: Folk, people

Voll Hoffnung, für Freiheit, für Brot: Full of hope, for freedom, for bread

Wehrt euch!: Defend yourselves!

Wunderbar: Wonderful

Zeitung: Newspaper

Zoologischer Garten: Zoological garden

Zwei: Two